Sleep with the Wolf
Walk with the Bear

A Novel by
CAROLYN CHEATHAM

Edited by Amy Ammons Garza

Cover Art
Doreyl Ammons Cain

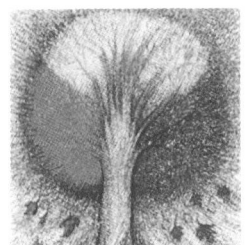

AMMONS COMMUNICATIONS, LTD.
64 Windsong Lane, Whittier, NC 28789

COPYRIGHT © 1998 BY CAROLYN CHEATHAM
ALL RIGHTS RESERVED.

First Edition

PUBLISHED BY:

AMMONS COMMUNICATIONS, LTD.
64 WINDSONG LANE, WHITTIER, NC 28789
PHONE & FAX 1-828-631-9203

LIBRARY OF CONGRESS CATALOG CARD NUMBER: 98-73876

ISBN: 0-9651232-4-3

I would like to acknowledge those who have given me support and encouragement in this endeavor.

My heartfelt thanks go to:

MY PARENTS
E.H. & Laura Miller

and

Andrew Ball
A dear, dear friend

With the help of these beautiful people, I found the courage to write my story.

Carolyn Cheatham

Carolyn Cheatham, born and raised in a farming community of the Ohio Valley, spent most of her young adult life in and around Titusville, Florida involved with the space program and working in the medical field. With her seven children grown and fulfilling a life long dream, she migrated to the Southern Appalachians in 1986. Currently her home is outside of Franklin, North Carolina, where she lives in a small cabin deep in the forest with four dogs and two cats.

Author's Note:

This is a true story of one woman's spiritual journey. As with many women reaching middle age, she felt as if she was on the down hill side of her life, only to find herself on an upward climb to a rebirth. I dedicate this book to all women, of all nations, no matter their age.

—*Carolyn Cheatham*

CHAPTER 1

SISTER WOLF, BROTHER BEAR...LOST IN MY SHADOW, I DID NOT HEAR YOUR FOOTSTEPS. WERE YOU THE WHISPERS I HEARD IN THE NIGHT? WERE YOU THE RUSTLE IN THE TREES? HAVE YOU BEEN WITH ME ALL MY LIFE?

From as far back as Annie could remember, she had felt incomplete. With that feeling growing stronger every passing year, she turned her back on a failing marriage, packed her few belongings and her old dog in her pickup truck, gathered what money she could, and kissed her children, grandchildren and parents goodbye. She left with the breeze blowing on her face.

Fear and loneliness gathered in her deepest being as she drove north, yet there grew at the same time a surprising excitement. She knew, then, she was doing the right thing.

Looking back later, she would see that she had not been in control of any of it anyway. And suddenly, a force stronger then she had ever known began pulling her toward an unknown destination.

After a few days of travel, Annie's gaze came to rest upon snow-covered mountains. There they were, the Smokies in all their splendor, welcoming her with their beauty. As she entered their majesty, a sense of peace which she had never before known enveloped her.

The mountain town of Franklin, North Carolina stretched before her, beckoning with its rolling landscape. Annie found a small apartment on the south end of town and began to explore her new surroundings. She strapped on a tattered old backpack, called to her dog and began each new day climbing a different mountain. The beauty made her heart race! She felt young and alive again.

With the years of caretaking behind her, she reveled in this newfound freedom. She spent the next few months outside in the wilderness of the Smoky Mountains, soaking up their medicine. And then, one day while roaming through Cowee Mountain range, Annie came upon a dirt road she did not know. Thinking it would carry her over the mountain, she turned off the main thoroughfare and headed up the narrow gravel lane. Trees and laurel reached out, touching the truck as she passed. Up, up, up she went. Suddenly, around a curve she came upon a place where the road split.

Annie stopped to consider which direction to take. Directly in front of her, between the roads, stood a cabin. Nestled in the cove, surrounded by deep woods, the structure seemed to be a part of the very nature that claimed it. A "For Sale" sign hugged the empty dwelling. Annie knew immediately she was home. She sensed that she had not found it, but that it had found her. Within days she had purchased the cabin and settled in. With only one bedroom, a living room combined with a kitchen area, and little possessions, the move took no time at all.

However, with the move came new challenges. An old pot-bellied stove, the cabin's only heat, required a new learning experience. She would have to buy a chain saw and put up her own wood for the coming winter. And she would learn how to live alone on the side of this lonesome mountain.

The days that followed were routine. Annie busied herself attending to a new garden and caring for the stray dogs and cats that had found their way to her door.

Spring died into summer. With the weather warmer, Annie felt a compulsion to familiarize herself with her new surroundings. The mountain behind her cabin seemed to be calling to her, so one morning she set off, climbing into what was to become the beginning of a wash of adventure.

The only trails were those made by the wild animals, who did not seem to mind her presence. The terrain proved to be difficult, and a few times she thought of turning back, yet her mind forced her to continue.

Reaching the top and letting her instincts guide her, she turned to the right on the ridge line. After a few minutes of walking on what she guessed was an old overgrown logging road, she spotted a large outcropping of boulders. Scaling the tallest boulder, she raised herself and gazed around. The view made her a bit lightheaded; she wished she could spread her arms and soar down into the river valley. The river, thousands of feet below, sparkled and ran peacefully in the brilliant sun.

Letting her mind empty itself of the daily thoughts of survival, she drank in the beauty that lay before her. She sank to the granite gray of the boulder and rested. Time passed quickly. However, when the sun had marched further to the west, she knew she must begin her descent. She rose to leave.

Suddenly, three red-tailed hawks rose from the valley below. As she watched, within her mind came the words, "We have been sent to you as messengers and guides for the time when you will need us most. Hear us well. Go in peace."

Each hawk cried once in its own voice, soared high into the sky and disappeared into the distance.

Annie felt no fear and she did not question what had just happened. The breezes of evening grew colder, but she felt only warmth and peace. Descending the mountain, which now seemed to be her own, she headed for home.

CHAPTER 2

YOUR LIFE IS IN TRANSFORMATION. I HAVE HEARD YOUR PLEA. I WILL GUIDE YOU TO ONE OF GREAT WISDOM. HEAR HIM WELL!
—*Grandmother*

Annie believed that peoples' lives were planned before birth; that, throughout life, spiritual guides were given. Native Americans referred to such guides as "the ancient ones," "the old ones" or "the ancestors." Annie believed that guides, by any name, were sent from God to help on life's pathway.

As she walked, many questions raced through her mind. "Why was I guided here at this time in my life? What do the three hawks mean? Do I have a mission? Why do these mountains seem to speak to me?"

As if in answer to these thoughts, Annie began to experience the nurturing of the gentle arms of the mountains that now surrounded her. Even the earth beneath her feet seemed to speak to her. In the quiet of the woods, voices from deep within her rose...voices she immediately knew to be of her Native American ancestors. Every fiber within her cried out, "Grandmother, help me! Show me the path to the knowledge I need."

At this time in her life, she desperately needed to fulfill her desire to know more of her ancestry; to know her very reason for living. Her instincts told her that she needed a mentor...one who could teach her the old ways. And then, one day Annie's prayer was answered.

"He's just the person you need to talk to," her friend Ramona had said. "He's an Elder of the Cherokee. His wisdom is revered by many. He and his wife live in the Snowbird Community.

"How do you know him?" Annie asked.

"I deliver supplies to him and his wife. They're quite old and have no vehicle to come down off the mountain."

"Do you think he would speak with me?" Annie swallowed nervously.

"I don't know...but I can ask." Ramona smiled encouragingly at her friend. "I'm scheduled to go next Wednesday. I'll just find out!"

Annie received a call from her friend on Wednesday evening. "He'll see you tomorrow!" Ramona's voice showed her excitement. "Remember! When you go, show respect for him. He's an Elder!"

The Elder's log cabin smelled of wood smoke and drying herbs. As Annie stood in the entrance, apprehension filled her. She knew the Elder still lived and believed in the old ways of the Native American; she did not want to offend him by asking the wrong questions. Out of this respect, she knew instinctively not to speak until the Elder opened the conversation. He waved his hand for her to sit on the stool before him. Quietly, she sat, her eyes respectfully down.

In the dimness, she felt him study her. Suddenly, in a strong but gentle voice, he asked,

"What do you wish from me?"

His question startled Annie and her mind went blank. Regaining her composure she found herself gazing into beautiful slightly faded eyes full of wisdom. In that moment, his gaze slit the outer shell of her person and entered her soul.

CHAPTER 3

I WILL HELP YOU TO UNDERSTAND. YOU MUST LISTEN WITH YOUR HEART. BUT FIRST YOU WILL GO ON A JOURNEY TO PREPARE.

—*The Elder*

Annie quivered at the importance of her answer to the Elder's question. She didn't want him to think of her as someone there just to interview him. Her answer must come from her heart.

"I must know who I am! My ancestors are of Cherokee blood. I know I've been called home, but I don't know why!" Annie spoke earnestly, continuing on with what had happened on the mountain. As she told of the three hawks, she watched his reaction closely. She had not told anyone else for fear of being called "crazy."

The Elder showed no signs of surprise, nor did he look

as if he felt that what she was saying was not normal. He only smiled and asked her to continue speaking. Annie could see in his eyes that he understood.

Rising from his large old rocker, the Elder gazed out of the window for many moments at the blue-hazed mountains. The expression on his face showed he was seeing and hearing something that Annie could not.

Finally, he turned to her and said, "I will help you to understand, but you must listen with your heart and not with your ears. You must listen both to me and your guides. You have neither been blessed nor cursed with this obligation which has been passed to you. Someone, somewhere in the world carried it before you, but has left the earth. For reasons known only to God, you, along with others of the living, are to learn the past which will be the future. Your obligation is to pass these teachings on to others. Some will try not to hear you, but you must do your best.

"You were brought here because this is the land of your ancestors. You carry the blood of the Native American from your Mother which, as we believe, is the strongest side. You were raised in the white world and never taught the ways of our world. You had to grow, you had to experience life, both good and bad, before you were ready to accept the teachings. Is it not true that all your life there was a part of you that had no meaning--a void, so to speak?"

Annie was taken aback by that statement. How did he know?

"You will be tested many times. Your faith and strength will, at times, fall along the path. It will be up to you to pick yourself up and continue even when those around you ridicule you and try to prove you wrong."

The Elder sat down and seemed to doze off. Annie, taking this as a sign, rose to leave. As she reached the door he spoke in a very soft and somewhat dreamy voice. "Go back to your mountain; stay three days and three nights, bring nothing with you except water. You may build a fire, but take no food until the morning of the fourth day. The three hawks will send guides to you. Do not be afraid of them for they are your brothers. Return to me following this quest."

CHAPTER 4

WE HAVE BEEN BROUGHT TOGETHER AS SISTERS. WE HAVE GIVEN A PIECE OF OUR SPIRIT TO EACH OTHER. WE THANK YOU FOR YOUR VOW.

—*The Deer*

Annie went straight home and threw into her backpack an old warm blanket, some matches and water. She then crawled into her bed until first light when she would begin her ascent to the mountain.

The day broke as usual with mist covering the mountain, but she had no trouble finding her way. When she had almost reached the top, the sun broke through the mist, revealing a cobalt sky. A soft gentle breeze caressed her face. By midday, she had climbed out onto the overhanging boulder.

Now, warmed by the sun, she longed to stretch out and

take a nap. But there was work to be done before nightfall. She gathered wood for her evening fire, and leaves and pine boughs for a sleeping mat. Wait! Did the Elder say she was permitted to sleep? She wasn't sure, but she would try to stay awake. The air cooled as evening fell. Annie lit her fire, wrapped her blanket around her shoulders and settled in for whatever was to come.

The sun had long since gone to his western home and the first stars began to show themselves. An owl called in the distance and other night birds made their presence known. Although Annie could hear the night creatures moving through the woods, she felt no fear. Since there was no moon, the night was very dark. Building up the fire, she lay back on her mat and gazed into one of the most beautiful skies she had ever seen.

Annie wondered about the hawks. They had not been there to greet her. "Maybe the time was not right," she mused. "They will know." She waited, letting her mind roam free, but nothing happened. She caught herself dozing off from time to time through the night. She awoke hungry, but knew she must force that thought from her mind. The Elder had said "No food."

With dawn Annie's optimism began to wane, but here she was, and here she would stay. Upon rising, her back hurt, her legs cramped and the night's chill had seeped into her bones. She needed to walk off the aches and pains. Looking around, she spotted a game trail to her left. Following the trail, she found fresh deer tracks which were common on the mountain this time of year. She followed the tracks. Before long, she came upon a doe and her fawn. Annie was downwind and quiet, so the deer did not sense her presence.

Annie loved observing wildlife in their natural surroundings and this is just what she needed this morning to lift her spirits and warm her blood. They were so beautiful—the doe with a soft reddish-gray color and the fawn still carrying its spots. Annie sent a message with her mind to the doe: "I recognize you as a kindred spirit. I see you as my sister. I vow never to take your life or those of your kind for any purpose. Go in peace and care for your little one." Instantly, the doe stopped grazing and flicking her ears, turned in Annie's direction.

Annie froze, thinking the breeze had shifted and the doe had picked up her scent. However, since the deer did not bolt, Annie stepped out onto the trail. For a long moment, they stood only ten feet apart, gazing into each other's eyes. The doe and the woman, both mothers giving to one another a portion of their spirit. Then, Annie moved up the trail and the doe and fawn turned to go in the opposite direction. They parted with understanding and respect. Annie, looking skyward, whispered, "Thank you."

Annie returned to her boulder, settled herself down, drank a little water and watched the sun rise above the eastern mountains. Morning birds were awake and calling to one another, giving her a sense of being a real part of Mother Earth. Letting her mind drift, she thought of her past, her children and grandchildren. They were so caught up in the modern world of "hurry, hurry, hurry" that she wondered if they ever took the time to see and hear the real world. Remembering the doe and fawn, she felt blessed and wished her grandchildren could look away from their TV's, VCR's and video games long enough to witness the sights she had seen this morning. "Maybe someday," she thought, "maybe someday."

As the sun climbed higher into the sky warming Annie's body, she felt drowsy from lack of sleep. Stretching out on the warm boulder she began to drift off. In her sleepy mind's eye, she saw, or thought she saw, a deer. The deer spoke.

"Our kind was put on earth to help feed others," it said. "Once, long ago, we gave ourselves freely. Your kind respected and revered us. Our lives were never taken without asking for permission and forgiveness; nothing was wasted. But now we are hunted down, not just for food, but for sport and we are never shown respect. You vowed never to take our lives. We thank you for your promise. Even so, if you are ever really in need of food, one of us will present itself to you for your survival. Do not be afraid to break your vow. You have our permission."

Annie was jolted awake! She lay very still, trying to see or hear what had awakened her. Silence. She noticed her renewed spirit and, strangely, she no longer felt hungry.

The day passed into evening and, still, the hawks had not come to the mountain. She gave this a lot of thought while gathering more wood for her second night's fire. The air had changed. Looking to the northwest, Annie could see dark clouds building. Knowing the weather in the mountains could change very quickly, she hoped a strong storm would not catch her out in the open. As night approached, the clouds grew heavier but the rain held off. Aside from the cloud cover obscuring the stars, Annie's second night passed much like the first.

Daylight dragged its heels because of the heavy clouds. When the morning mist gave way to a drizzling cold rain, Annie's heart sank. "Am I being foolish?" she asked herself. "I am standing in the cold rain, on a mountain top, with no cover waiting for a message!"

After washing her face and hands in a small spring not far from her rock, she huddled in her damp blanket. Miserably, she concentrated on the river below. A voice spoke inside her head. "You want to go home, don't you?" it said. "But, this is a test and you are stronger than the tears you want to shed. Stop feeling sorry for yourself; look around for there is much to learn."

Encouraged, Annie threw off the damp blanket. She arose from the ground and, shaking herself like a wet dog, she began exploring. She found blackberry blossoms in full bloom. She stored them in her memory so she could return in the late summer to gather the sweet dark fruit. After walking for a couple of hours, she sat on a fallen log to watch a pair of birds fly in and out of a nest with mouths full of food. She didn't know what kind of birds they were, but noticed their devotion to their young. She thought about the state of the world, with all of its fighting and killing. If only humans could be as concerned about the survival of their species as animal species, man might have a chance. It seemed to her now that power, greed and, even "progress," would destroy humankind. What had the Elder said? "Learn the past for it will be the future."

Annie took a deep breath, telling herself, "Maybe mankind will listen and learn before it's too late. Perhaps the Elder was right; maybe I was given the obligation to try to change mankind's thinking. Even if I reach only a few people, I will have done something."

Although the rain had stopped, the clouds continued to hang low. This would be her last night on the mountain; she hoped it would not be a long one. As Annie returned to the boulder, she became angry with herself. She had not kept the wood dry for her evening fire! She knew better than this, for she had spent time in the woods most of her life. Camping with her family was one of her favorite memories. Her father had taught her the ways of the woods, so why was she not thinking straight?

Maybe the lack of food and sleep had dulled her mind,

but Annie considered this a poor excuse. Annie did not like it when people, including herself, made excuses for their own mistakes. "You are becoming a foolish old woman," she told herself. "After all, this is not the middle of January! You won't freeze to death without a fire." Yet, because she was wet to the skin, a fire would give her some comfort. After searching for a while, she found a handful of nearly dry tinder under a large oak tree. In a few moments and many matches, a small blaze reluctantly came to life. Even this small accomplishment made Annie's spirits rise a little. The rain did not return, and for this she was thankful. The warmth of the fire began to dry her clothing. As night came, the clouds parted and stars could be seen through the clear air. Such experiences made it impossible for Annie to imagine wanting to live anywhere else.

As she stared into her fire, she saw the face of the Elder. Looking out from hooded eyes, he spoke. "You have done as you were told. I would like to say you did well. You think nothing happened on this quest. Through the rest of this night you should relive each moment and give it a lot of thought. We will talk when you return to me." Then, his face faded, and Annie could not remember ever feeling so alone.

Doing as she was told, she tried to remember each event no matter how small. Remembering the doe and fawn was easy. The deer in her dream came clearly to her mind. The little birds feeding their young were there, too. The rain and discomfort, the joy and sadness, all were there.

That's it! She had experienced both joy and sadness in a short time. Was this another of life's lessons to draw from later? Was this what the Elder wanted her to see? Annie heard her mother's voice speaking to her. "Remember child...remember that without pain you cannot know pleasure." A smile crossed her lips. She could understand now.

As a small child the expression had not been much comfort.

The night passed quickly, though Annie did not sleep. With first light, she drowned her fire, disassembled her sleeping mat and rolled up her blanket. She left no sign that she had ever been there. This was a strict rule with Annie--when you break camp, leave nothing behind but footprints. Tired and hungry, she looked forward to a hot bath and a little food.

Three quarters of the way down the mountain, her dogs met her. It was good to see them, and, judging from the way they danced about her feet, they were glad to see her, too.

CHAPTER 5

MY EARTH WALK IS FINISHED. IT IS TIME FOR ME TO GO, LITTLE ONE. IF YOU ARE IN NEED OF ANYTHING, I WILL RETURN TO YOU.

—*Grandfather*

After having a bath and eating, Annie went to thank her neighbor for taking care of her animals during her time on the mountain. Once home, she fell into a deep and dreamless sleep. The following day she returned to the Elder's cabin. Remaining silent until he spoke proved difficult for her this time. She had so many questions! His first words were, "Tell me of your journey."

Not sure where to begin, Annie wondered if he wanted to know every detail of what happened, or just her thoughts during her stay. Before beginning her story, she had to know one important thing. She asked, "Why did the hawks not come to the mountain?"

Smiling that broad, beautiful smile that seemed to come so easily to him, he said, "Why should they come? They did not call for you. I sent you to the mountain. It was time for you to look deep into yourself; to see your strengths and your weaknesses. Did you find those?"

"I'm not sure," Annie replied, revealing a little disappointment in her voice. "I guess I was expecting more."

"What did you think was going to happen?" he asked. "Did you think you were going to have a great vision that could save the world?"

Annie started to speak, "No, but ...."

Raising a hand, palm out, he stopped her. Speaking softly he explained. "This is all new to you and you have much to learn. The smallest things will not seem important, but you will soon realize that everything has a purpose. Now tell me what you saw, heard and thought."

Annie told of the great black sky with the many stars; of the doe and the fawn; of her vow; and of the deer in her dream, if it was, indeed, a dream. At this he said, "Does it matter if it was a dream or not? The deer, giver of life to the Native Americans for many, many generations, saw you as one who respects all creatures that belong to our Mother Earth, and he spoke true to you."

She told of the birds, of her thoughts on the future of mankind, of the damp and cold, of her mistakes, her hunger, his face in her fires, and her loneliness.

After she was finished speaking, he looked at her for a long time. Then with a firm, but loving voice, he said, "I told you of the many tests that would be put before you, not only by others but also by yourself. These, perhaps, will be the hardest to pass."

Then he explained, "Each of us, every man, woman and child has ancient memories, knowledge left to us from our ancestors. Most people of the modern world are not aware that these memories are locked away somewhere in their minds. We must be willing to see them as truth and not try to rework them to fit our personal lives. Think on this. Your spirituality is strong. This will help, for you must teach yourself to hear the words of those who have gone before you. No one else can take you into your own mind. Listen well. I remind you again, learn the past, for the past will be the future."

Annie thanked the Elder for his patience with her and left.

On her drive home, the last words the Elder had spoken to her kept reverberating through her mind. Annie felt that he had referred to a time even before her grandparents' birth--a time when man and nature were as one, when love and respect were shown to Mother Earth and all of her children, man and beast alike.

Back at the cabin Annie felt drained, but since she could not rest, she walked to the river. The sun was high and warm; the river sang its quiet song. Stretching out on its grassy bank, Annie thought of her grandfather. They had been very close to each other, and she remembered the day he died. She had received a call at her cabin at 4 am telling her of his passing. She had been deeply saddened; yet she knew her grandfather would always be with her.

That morning—the morning of her grandfather's death—Annie had been called to the mountain. At the top, there they were...the hawks! They circled her three times and left. And, turning, her heart leapt, for there on the rock beside her sat her grandfather.

The two of them spent the day talking of time gone by on the family farm. They laughed and cried, and Annie's heart expanded, no longer broken. Finally, taking her hand in his, he said, "It is time for me to go, little one, but if you are in need of anything, I will return to you." And with that, he climbed off the boulder, walked up the trail and disappeared.

Like her mother, always in control of her emotions, Annie did not cry easily. On this night, however, the tears came in great floods. She did not fight them; for she knew grieving held a cleansing process for the heart and soul.

Annie had decided she would not attend the funeral, for to her it was a ceremony allowing the living to say goodbye. She had no need to say goodbye. Her grandfather still lived in her heart. Annie did not believe physical death was the end. At the time, she prayed her parents, who had always been loving and supportive, would understand. She wanted to celebrate his life, not his death. As long as all her grandparents' blood flowed in the veins of those coming after, their heritage would live on.

Returning to the present, Annie sat up, stretched and rose to leave the river. Spotting a fisherman on the other side, she acknowledged him with a wave of her hand. He smiled and waved back. Turning, she entered the woods, and headed back to her cabin. Walking home, she thought of how lucky she was to be living in such a beautiful place. The people were friendly; the climate good most of the time; and she could visit the town eleven miles away or roam the woods and feel safe. She had so much for which to be thankful. She didn't live in a fancy house or drive a new car or wear expensive clothes. She had no jewels or fine china. She did not have a great mind or great beauty. But what she had was worth more than any of these. She had her health; she had known the love of a man; she had beautiful, healthy children and grandchildren; and she had loving parents and grandparents. Her garden gave her vegetables, the woods gave her roots and berries, the river gave her fish. More than this, she had her freedom--freedom to choose her own way of life--a gift which many people in other parts of the world had never known.

Though she had a few friends and would do what she could to help anyone in need, Annie realized that she was gradually turning her back on society. She had grown weary of advertisements telling her she had to have this or that to be happy. As she explored her new life, she realized, most of all, that she had permitted herself to be controlled by others, to think as they wanted her to think, to do as they wanted her to do. Now it seemed the ancients were showing her a simpler, more humane way to live.

CHAPTER 6

YOU AND YOU ALONE ARE RESPONSIBLE FOR YOUR OWN ACTIONS. WE ARE BORN KNOWING RIGHT FROM WRONG. THE ANCIENTS HAVE SEEN TO THIS!

—The Elder

Summer moved along with warm days and cool nights. Some nights, she would sleep out on the porch. Drifting off, she'd hear the owls, crickets and spring frogs singing from the banks of the stream that ran beside her cabin. Peace filled her as she slept within nature's music--a symphony that could not be duplicated by man.

Annie returned to the mountain several times through the summer; sometimes on her own, and sometimes when the hawks called her. When she felt physically or spiritually out of balance, the mountain had a way of bringing her back to center. It had become her favorite place to meditate. For Annie, to pray was to talk to God; to meditate was to listen to God. She felt the need to talk less and listen more.

The three hawks were God's messengers to her and became a strong force in her life. Most of her friends and family did not understand, so they scoffed at her beliefs. The Elder had spoken the truth: her faith would be tested. She had to admit there were times she questioned it herself. At these times, however, something always happened to bring her back to certainty.

As time went on, the Elder called often for her. She took advantage of this and asked him for answers to the questions that suddenly filled her mind. He answered most of them, but more often then not, he forced her to look deeper into her ancient memories and find the answers herself.

"You, and you alone, are responsible for your own actions," he would say. He had no use for those who blamed their parents, or society for their own evil ways. "We are born knowing right from wrong. The ancients have seen to this and blaming others is just an excuse. There will always be evil forces among us. Each of us has evil thoughts at times, but putting these thoughts into actions will throw you off balance."

He grew silent for a long time, looking deep into Annie's eyes. Outside the wind came in a sudden gust, making Annie jump, then became calm.

"You have the instinct to control," he said. "This is something you must learn to put to rest; it is not good. You must learn to just 'BE!' For many, many years now mankind has felt he must control his world. When this is done, the earth is no longer in balance, and the Great Mother fights back to protect all her children. You have learned that you are neither higher nor lower than any living thing on earth. You are learning to see everything as an equal--to see that each has a purpose for the balance of the world. Mankind was not created to rule others as he wishes to do. He was meant to live in harmony with all."

Smiling as if he knew a secret, he added, "Sometimes I wonder if God feels he made a mistake with humans. For instance, wolves live in a social group. Everything the wolf does is done for the strength and survival of the group. Although mankind lives in a social group, man wants to know 'What's in it for me?,' before he does anything.

Then the Elder told the story of a tribe of hunters across the sea who had gone out to find meat for the village. "They came upon a large elephant," he said. "They asked the elephant for forgiveness and permission to take its life, which it gave. All the hunters threw their spears at the same time but only one found its true mark, killing the large beast. Attaching strong vine ropes to the carcass, the hunters started back to their village. To make the difficult job easier, they began chanting, 'We have meat for our children, we have meat for our old ones, we have meat for all. Our elephant, our elephant, our elephant,' they chanted.

"Soon, the hunter whose spear had made the kill, spoke saying, 'My spear made the kill,' and he began chanting, 'my elephant, my elephant, my elephant.' That's when the rest of the hunters dropped their ropes and left the man to try to drag the beast home alone. Since the one hunter could not do this task, no one would have meat for their children."

The Elder then went to his window and gazed out for a long time. Finally, turning to Annie he said, "Time is coming when we will once again live in groups or villages to survive. Everyone will work together to grow food and build shelters. Everyone will care for the children and the old ones. No one will be able to survive without the others. This time is coming, child, so prepare yourself, your children, your grandchildren and anyone else who will open their eyes and ears to see and hear what I have seen and heard from my guides. Humans lived this way before; it was good."

Annie, now standing at the window with him, whispered, "The past will be the future."

Looking at her out of the corner of his eye, he said, "Exactly."

CHAPTER 7

I SAW HER STANDING ON THE MOUNTAIN. SHE LOOKED COLD AND IN FEAR. SHE WAS NOT AWARE OF ME. I KNEW SHE NEEDED MY FUR TO HELP HER LIVE.

—Sister Wolf

It was late summer when Annie began preserving food from her garden. She had gathered wild cherries, raspberries, blackberries, and any other wild fruit she could find. She made jams and jellies. She knew how good these would taste when the trees grew bare and the snow drifted past the windows. Farmers had let her gather the odd ears of corn left in their fields by the pickers. Annie stored this corn for the birds and other wild animals struggling to find food when the snows covered the earth.

As the trees began to change from green to vivid red,

yellow and orange, Annie knew it was time to gather nuts for the winter. Walking the river bank, she gathered black walnuts, butternuts, hickory nuts and chestnuts. Squirrels fussed at her from the trees.

"Do not fuss so, Little Brother," she said smiling. "I will take only what I need. I will leave plenty for you and your family." They seemed to understand, and sat watching her with their little front feet drawn to their chests.

This was Annie's favorite time of year. The cool, crisp air made her want to be out of doors twenty-four hours a day. The sky seemed bluer, the stars clearer, and the air cleaner than at any other time of year. Mother Earth was preparing her children for winter. They were putting on fat, growing heavier coats, and feeding heartily to survive the cold winter nights.

Annie, too, must prepare. Since she could not grow a heavier coat, heat for her cabin was the answer. She roamed the deep woods, checking dead trees for nests before cutting them for firewood. She did not want to destroy the homes of the squirrels, woodpeckers and raccoons who used dead trees for winter homes. Cut, split, stack. Cut, split, stack. It was backbreaking work, but it was the kind of work that made her glad to be alive. Mornings would leave frost diamonds for her in the cove, across the fields, upon the backs of cattle, and along the edges of the river.

The people who came to the mountains for the warm summer months were gone now, and Annie grew both sad and glad to see them go. She enjoyed their company, but also needed her solitude. She was happiest being 'Inagehi' (In naw geh hee), a Cherokee word meaning, 'a person who lives alone in the wilderness.' During the months when so many people were in the mountains, the wild animals stayed away, and she missed them. The only time she really felt at peace came when she roamed the woods, visited her mountain, or enjoyed the presence of the Elder. Life beyond these woods moved too fast for Annie. Her new grandchildren were being born, and though she was pleased to know that her blood line would continue, she wondered and worried about their quality of life. She asked God and the Ancients to watch over her grandchildren.

"Old Cold Maker" made his way down the mountains each night, with temperatures dropping to freezing and below. As "Sun Boy" rose each day, he pushed "Cold Maker" back for a few hours. Sooner or later, "Cold Maker" would win for a time, as he had for centuries during this cycle of the earth. The Great Mother needed her rest.

With her summer and fall work finished, Annie now had more time to spend on her mountain or at the river close to her cabin. One cold, sunny day, she felt the need to roam in new territory. She couldn't explain this urge, and so she let herself experience a sense of adventure. Dragging out an old map, she planned a new route for that day's walk. A spot on the map kept drawing her attention. Studying it closer, she saw that since it now belonged to the National Forest, she needn't be concerned about trespassing on private property. She also noted that, at one time, there had been a village of some type in the area. The map did not indicate when the village might have been inhabited. It could have been a white village or an Indian village, or both. Her best judgment placed it at forty-five minutes to an hour's drive from her home. She filled a day pack with water and a light lunch, and started her old pickup truck. As usual, Annie prayed that the truck would get her there and back. Lately, Annie had been allowing at least one of her dogs to accompany her on her walks. Today, however, something told her to leave the dogs home and go alone.

Annie parked her truck on an abandoned logging road and began climbing. The day was clear but cool, with a light breeze coming from the North. Annie felt strong and clear-headed. She found herself surrounded by a hardwood forest with little undergrowth. The only trails she found were well-used game trails. She moved slowly and quietly, hoping to catch a glimpse of some of the animals. By noon she had broken out of the dense forest, and onto a field of grass dried by nightly freezes. On a small, sun-warmed boulder, she removed her pack and sat facing south, watching the woods below for movement. Since wildlife wintered on the south side of the mountains, this view was her best chance to see them. Before long, two young bucks stepped into view. They grazed on what little vegetation lingered at this higher elevation. Annie did not move. She scarcely breathed. The deer moved closer, then saw her. They threw their heads up, standing as still as Annie. It was their turn to watch her, but not for long. They showed no fear, and really no interest. They returned to their grazing, and slowly moved away. Annie suddenly realized she had not been breathing and caught her breath, her lungs crying out for oxygen.

After a couple of deep breaths, and a moment to let her muscles relax, she decided to further investigate the mountain. She felt a lot of energy here. This place held power! Could it have been a spiritual site for those who had been here before? The longer she stayed, the stronger the power grew. Because she did not know this mountain as well as she knew her own, she kept track of the sun's path across the sky. She did not want to descend the mountain after dark, and risk getting lost. But the day was still young, so she moved further from the game trail she had been following. Squirrels scolded, and birds hopped from tree limb to tree limb, watching her movements. Annie found signs of deer and bear. She saw where wild turkey and grouse had been feasting on hickory nuts. With the sun against her back, Annie realized that her shadow had grown longer. It was time to begin her descent from the mountain. Since it wasn't far to her truck, Annie decided to first rest awhile. She made a pallet of leaves, and lay back watching the fluffy clouds overhead. Small patches of sun warmed her.

Before long, she felt herself drifting off, but decided that a brief nap would be all right. She soon had a dream so vivid that it was like watching a movie. In the dream, she stood as an old woman, hauntingly cold under a dark sky. Fear raged through every fiber of her body. She found herself facing the vast wilderness completely alone. A light mist began to rise, hugging the arms of the bushes and trees around her. And then, from out of the dim white of the fog, a large grey-white wolf lumbered toward her, the swish of her body stirring the gray sea with her presence. The she-wolf's yellow eyes showed no malice. The woman experienced no fear. The wolf spoke to her, "I will lie beside you and warm your body until light of day; then I will guide you back to your people." Then, the wolf and the woman slept, their bodies curled.

As Annie slowly awoke, she noticed that the sun had dropped behind the mountains, and the temperature had also dropped. The cold evening fanned about her, but Annie felt none of it. The leaves around her were warm. She opened her clenched hand, and there lying across her palm was a tuft of grey-white fur. Her eyes sought the ground where she had lain, and found the same fur mingled with the leaves and twigs. She could no longer be sure whether she had been dreaming. Was it a vision? Since there were no longer any wolves living in these mountains, from where did the fur come? It was real--or was it? She could feel it, see it, and smell it--couldn't she? She pushed the fur deep into her jeans pocket. If it was still there when she arrived home, she would show it to the Elder; he would know. Anyone else would laugh at her. She did not want to leave this place, but since she was not prepared to stay for the night, she reluctantly returned to her truck and headed home. She did not look back, for she knew nothing would be there.

When Annie arrived at the cabin, her dogs whined, whimpered, and shied away from her. Why? Then it occurred to her. Was it still there--that tuft of fur she had pushed into her pocket? Reaching deep, she could feel the soft fur, but she did not draw it out. The scent of wolf was the cause of her dogs' anxious behavior. Leaving the dogs outside, she placed the fur in a small plastic bag to contain the scent. Tomorrow she would go to the Elder; right now, she needed a shower and some rest.

The following morning, Annie retrieved the tuft of fur from the plastic bag. She tied it tightly in a small strip of leather and headed for the Elder's cabin. She knew it was proper to always present a small gift to an Elder, such as a small lovely stone, food, or firewood, and on this day she did not have to think about a gift. The gift was here in her pocket, tied with a strip of leather.

The Elder welcomed her in silence, as he always did, and studied her for some time, as he always did. Finally, he spoke. "You are a troubled woman," he observed. "What lies heavy in your heart?"

She told him of her visit to a mountain where she had felt the mountain's power and spirit. She told him of the warmth of the dream. She then drew out of her pocket the tuft of fur, and handing it to him with shaking hands, she said no more. Part of Annie's mind feared that the Elder would not believe what she had told him; yet, she had never lied to him, and he knew that. He looked at the fur for a long time, holding it gently in his hands. With his eyes closed, he said softly, "I know the mountain of which you speak, and you are right. It does hold great power. It is very much alive with the spirits of those who have gone before us. Once, it was there that prayers were offered to our Creator. I was told of this mountain by my grandfather. In my younger days, I visited it often to offer my prayers. In your dream, you were taken into the past. For a short time, you were given the spirit of the woman in the dream. I have no doubt that the wolf did protect her from death on the night of which you speak."

Now Annie felt really confused. How could she be taken back to another time, and still wake with a handful of fur? She asked this question of the Elder. His eyes showed a touch of anger directed at her. She knew immediately that she was wrong in questioning the spirits and what they had shown her. Even though she knew she was wrong, the Elder reprimanded her, telling her not to return to that mountain until she could accept its gifts without question.

He softened the edges of his words and eyes with a smile. "Are you beginning to understand?" he asked.

"I think so," Annie replied, "but I'm not sure."

The Elder chuckled and waved his hand as if waving a gnat away from his face. "Oh My!" he said. "Mankind is always looking for logical explanations, as a part of you is doing now. Sometimes I wonder why I even bother with you at all."

When Annie saw that he was still smiling, she knew he was not speaking in anger, but was teasingly making a point. He continued, "Questions, questions! You and your questions! Have you not learned anything? I have been trying to teach you, among other things, that there are some things you must accept without question. The spirits of your ancestors know what they are doing, and you should receive their gifts with gratitude, instead of your foolish questions!"

His voice was becoming angry again, but he caught himself. Taking a deep breath, he said, "You may not know the reason for this wolf's fur, but the answer will be given to you. All you have to do is open your mind and let it in."

Annie started to speak, but then she hesitated. This was the first time he had become angry with her, and she was a little hurt. She had grown to love this wise and beautiful old man, and she only wanted to be worthy of him. Looking over at him, she saw that his shoulders were slumped a little, and she knew he was tired.

She rose, touching him on his shoulder, speaking softly. "Another day."

He replied with a shake of his head. When she reached the door, he called to her. "Wait! Your tuft of fur."

Without turning around, Annie said, "I wish you to have it."

"Why?" he asked.

Turning and looking directly into his eyes, she smiled. "Now it is you who ask too many questions, Grandfather."

The drive home was pleasant, even though Annie still felt a little hurt over the Elder's anger. Deep down, she knew he was only trying to make her understand. Their relationship had become more then teacher-student. Annie felt the Elder really cared for her as a member of his family. He had excepted her, sharing his valuable time. And not only was he teaching her how to look at the world a little differently, but how she could see herself differently. She was proud of some of the things she saw in herself. She gave credit for these things to her parents. For that which she felt no pride--the aspects of her life that needed work--she took personal responsibility. Beyond these lessons, the Elder also taught Annie the old ways of the Indian. These were teachings she especially enjoyed. She found that the old beliefs held more credibility with her than those of the so-called "modern" world.

CHAPTER 8

OUR SPIRITS, AND THE SPIRITS OF OUR ANCESTORS HAVE BEEN JOINED. THE CREATOR HAS SEEN TO THIS. DO NOT FEAR ME, FOR I AM YOUR BROTHER.

—*Brother Bear*

Winter arrived with a vengeance. Old Cold Maker had won. Snows were light, but the cold crept in bitter and unforgiving. Because Annie's cabin sat distant from any main roads, she stocked extra supplies. She knew if the snow covered her route to the road, it would be difficult to get out. That much snow was rare in the Southern Appalachians, but since harsh winters had occurred before, it would be foolish not to prepare for the possibility. Her wood supply was good, and her small cabin held heat well. With preparations made, she felt confident she would be ready to meet the winter. The old wood burning stove became the focal point, not only for her, but also for her many animals, who lay around the stove on cold, windy winter nights.

The forest became very quiet in winter, and the slightest sound could easily be heard. Once the tourists and summer residents left the woods, wildlife moved about more freely. It was not unusual to hear the animals as they roamed the woods during the day.

One cold and very still night, Annie had an unexpected visitor. Inside the cabin Annie had curled up with a good book, when suddenly her dogs growled deep in their chests. Usually only barkers to let her know when people were near—never had she heard this kind of growling. She picked up the large flashlight she kept by the door. As the door squeaked open, she expected the dogs to charge past her into the night. But they did not. They stayed behind her, emitting the same low, deep growls.

"Some protectors you are!" she whispered to them, as she stepped out onto the porch alone. Sweeping the beam of light toward the front yard and down the lane, Annie saw nothing unusual. Still on the porch, she turned off the flashlight and closed the cabin door behind her, listening for sounds that would reveal the source of the dogs' behavior. Against the backdrop of silence, she thought she heard breathing other than her own, which had become more rapid. Her heart seemed to rise into her throat. Defying her fear, she forced her moccasined feet off the porch and around to the side of the cabin. The breathing now closer, and she sensed a musky odor. She turned on the flashlight, directed it toward the sound, and caught her breath sharply! She was face to face with a black bear! The bear, as startled as Annie, stared at her and both of them froze. Surprised to see a bear away from his den on such a cold night, she decided not to ponder why. Her fear subsided when she remembered that black bears are not known for aggressive behavior toward humans.

She opened her mouth to speak, but caught herself. She did not want to scare the bear further. At the same time, she realized her beam of light shone directly into the bear's eyes, blinding him. She lowered the light so its glow engulfed both her and the bear. Then, they stood and gazed at each other for what seemed to be an eternity as his eyes flashed in the shadows. Did she imagin that he seem to be telling her something? Finally, the animal turned and began walking back into the woods. As the bear became a dark shadow moving among the trees in the light of the half-moon, Annie could not be sure whether she shivered from the cold or from the excitement of being so close to a bear. As she entered the cabin, she chuckled at the sight of her dogs, laying curled up and sound asleep, as if nothing had happened.

"Don't bother to get up!" she told them. "I took care of the situation. Remind me someday to look for a good guard dog!"

It had been over a week since Annie had seen the Elder. He had not called for her, and she was becoming concerned about him. The sky clear with no snow in the forecast, she drove to his cabin. As before, the Elder's wife opened the door in silence, and retreated to the kitchen. Annie had often wondered about the old woman, but it was not polite to ask too many questions about another's household. Annie just smiled and nodded toward the woman when she entered. The Elder was sitting in his rocker with what appeared to be a new blanket wrapped around his shoulders. The fire blazed in the fireplace and the cabin was warm. The Elder waved his hand toward a chair across from him; Annie instantly relaxed and sat down.

"Always the same," she thought to herself. "I guess it is true that familiarity does breed contentment."

After the Elder opened the conversation, Annie commented on the beauty of the blanket. His face showed pride when he told her his nephew had sent it from Oklahoma.

"A gift!" he exclaimed, with pride.

"It is a worthy gift," Annie answered. They talked of the weather and how much snow they may get before spring.

Rubbing his hands, he said, "My old bones can no longer fight off the cold as they once could, and I miss hunting in new fallen snow." With a sigh, he continued, "Now I sit in front of my fire and let it speak to me."

Annie's heart ached for him, for growing old is both a blessing and a curse. With age comes wisdom, but also a feeling of uselessness.

Annie told the Elder she had brought some wood and would stack it on the back porch before she left. He smiled and thanked her. No matter how small her gifts, he always thanked her.

Annie told him of her encounter a few nights before with the bear. He found the story to be amusing. She told it in detail, and, as the story unfolded, it became funnier even to Annie. When she told the part about the bear's eyes trying to tell her something, the Elder grew serious again.

"Do not underestimate the power of animals," he told her. "They know things long before humans do, and they carry great spirits. What he was telling you will be revealed to you at the right time. Again, I warn you not to question it."

"Why a bear, Grandfather?" she asked.

His eyes sparkled with laughter. "There you go again with your questions."

"I could see it and smell it," she said. "I did not try to touch it, though, and now, I wish I had."

"Well, no matter," he said. "I will answer your question. You have been sent two more guides in addition to the hawks and the deer."

"Two more?" she asked, wide-eyed.

"Have you so quickly forgotten the wolf?" he asked.

"No, but it wasn't real . . . not like the hawks, the deer, and now, the bear."

"Are you so sure?" he asked.

This was becoming more difficult all the time, she thought. "My logical mind tells me one thing, and then, my spiritual mind tells me something else. You are not helping, Grandfather," she told him. "I'm more confused about this than ever!"

Lifting his hands and eyes toward the heavens, he spoke, "Lord! Help me with this child of yours. She is so bullheaded!" To her, he said, "Go home now. You have much to think about, and snows will come tonight. I don't want you stranded here with me," he chuckled.

Annie stacked the wood from her truck onto the Elder's porch, then left. When she was a couple of miles from her lane, the first snow flakes began to fall.

"The old man is incredible!" she smiled.

CHAPTER 9

I GIVE TO YOU, MY ANIMAL RELATIVES, APPLES AND OTHER GIFTS TO SHOW YOU MY APPRECIATION FOR YOUR LIVES.

—Annie

Winter calmed and Annie roamed the woods. All nature sang in brown and grey, the mountains filled with winter beauty. Annie enjoyed climbing to higher elevations this time of year, because she could see further with the trees bare.

The bear did not return to her yard. On her walks, Annie would often find his footprints on muddy banks of a stream, or she would find fallen trees, turned and torn in his search for grubs. Now and then, she would take apples with her to place at the spots where she knew the deer and bears fed. She wanted to leave small gifts to show her appreciation for their lives. She felt sure that even wildlife enjoyed gifts from time to time.

With each visit to the Elder, Annie saw him grow weaker. He never complained. His smile, and even the twinkle in his eyes, flashed when he welcomed her. It had been two years since she began coming to him. With each visit, he would ask her about her grandparents, her parents, and her children. He knew she was proud of all of them, but he also seemed to understand her need for solitude.

Annie rarely asked anyone to walk with her on her trips into the woods or into the mountains. She brought only her dogs and one cat, who had become quite a trail cat. Charging ahead of her on the trail, she would find him lying on a rock in the sun. He would give her a look as if to say, "Well, it's about time you caught up." Then, off he would go again! When they reached their destination, the cat would again be waiting for her. As Annie was catching her breath, she once told him that if she had a four-wheel drive, like he did, she could keep up with him.

More snows fell in February and March, keeping Annie closer to home. But, at least once a week, she would reach the Elder's cabin, even if she had to walk part of the way. She had given him and his wife warm slippers for Christmas. The slippers were always on his feet, even when he did not know she was coming. That pleased her, because he showed pride in them, as he had in the blanket given to him by his nephew.

CHAPTER 10

I HAVE TAUGHT YOU HOW TO REACH YOUR ANCIENT MEMORIES. ASK YOUR GUIDES TO SHOW YOU THE PATH THAT IS RIGHT FOR YOU.

—The Elder

On a day in the early part of April, the Elder sent word for Annie to come to his cabin. A touch of fear struck her heart. She prayed his illness would not take him yet. When she entered the cabin, she grew surprised to see him seated on the floor, cross-legged and straight-backed, staring into his fire. This time, the old woman motioned her to sit down beside him. Annie did as the woman indicated, taking a cross-legged position, like the Elder. He did not look in her direction, seemingly unaware that Annie was there. Before long, however, he turned his body to face her, in such a fluid motion that Annie almost didn't detect. She, in turn, faced him; but her movements were clumsy compared to his. No words had yet been spoken, but the Elder must have seen the questioning look in Annie's eyes, for he shook his head and smiled.

"I called you here today, because I have a gift for you," he said. "This is the cycle of the earth when The Mother is awakening from her winter sleep. She is preparing to give birth. Everything is reborn in spring. You came to me, by calendar time, around two years ago, when you were also looking for a kind of rebirth." With a bit of laughter in his voice, he said, "I have been a good teacher; you have been a fair student. Now I believe you have reached a point where you will be able to seek out the answers for yourself. You are, by no means, ready to teach others. Your full wisdom has not yet been brought to the surface; that comes with age. Yet, in your own quiet way, I expect you to carry the teachings to others. Do not demand that they hear you; just live as you believe, and the message will get out there.

"Never stop seeking, never stop learning. When this happens, our brains are dead. The brain is a gift, and it is our responsibility to feed and care for it. Do not allow it to become clouded over with strong drink or drugs."

"I have taught you how to reach your ancient memories, and that is important, but you must also know how to perceive the world as it is now. Learn to sort out the truths from the non-truths. In other words, do not believe everything you hear, but open your mind and then ask the ancients to show you the path that is right for you. Do you understand, Granddaughter?"

Annie thought for a moment, then replied. "Yes, Grandfather."

The Elder had very seldom used Annie's given name, and had only begun calling her 'Granddaughter' a few months before. She was now accustomed to calling him 'Grandfather,' as a term of endearment.

"Well, enough of that," he said. "There is something else I wish to speak to you about. It is something about which you already have a great deal of knowledge, but I wish for you to take it further. As you know, our guides and the spirits of our ancestors come in many shapes and forms. Your guides have been given to you in the form of animals. You are now aware of this, are you not?"

"Yes, Grandfather," Annie replied.

"Here is what you are to do," the Elder continued. "Spend as much time as you can with animals, both domestic and wild. You should know that wild animals are not wild; they are only free. Remember that. Study them; learn to read them; learn their body language, their voices, their facial expressions, and their habits. Love and respect them and their ways. This you already do, I know."

The Elder grew quiet for a moment, watching Annie's face. Then, he spoke again. "To understand the messages they bring you, you must bring forth your own lost animal instincts. Man carried these instincts a long time ago, but with time, he let them go, because he thought they would no longer be needed. In most cases, this is true, but instinct was a gift given to ensure the survival of man. Those instincts are still there, lying dormant in our minds, and that is good. Still, you must find at least some of them again. It will be to your benefit to understand your guides better. Do you now feel that you are ready to meet that goal?"

"Yes, Grandfather," Annie said again. "I will try not to let you down."

The Elder replied, with an edge to his voice, "It will not be me you are letting down, but yourself."

Annie had not noticed that the old woman had entered the room carrying three cups of something hot and steaming. The aroma filled the small room, and her memory was taken back to her grandmother who enjoyed sassafras tea. The woman handed the Elder a cup, then handed one to Annie, and kept one for herself. She sat down beside her husband, gracefully taking the cross-legged position. Annie marveled at how bones so old could move with such grace. This was the first time she had ever been offered food or drink. Her time here was usually spent learning, and nothing more. Now she was sharing a cup of sassafras tea and sitting with these beautiful people. For the first time, she really looked at the old woman. Shorter than her instructor, with skin lighter than the Elder's but as deeply creased with wrinkles. Her snow white hair was worn in a bun at the back of her head. Annie looked into the old woman's eyes, and thought how beautiful they were. When she looked at her husband, love and admiration poured from those eyes. Annie would later learn that the Elder and his wife never had children. Maybe this was one reason their bond with each other was so strong.

Annie's attention was suddenly taken from the old woman to the voice of the Elder. He was saying something to his wife in the Cherokee language. Annie did not understand. His wife answered him and smiled, so Annie decided it must be a private joke -- why else would they speak in such a way? The Elder then spoke to Annie in English. The woman continued to direct her smile at Annie. What a warm, lovely smile, Annie thought; toothless, yet beautiful. She must have been a lovely young woman. It was hard to turn her attention back to the Elder. Annie wanted to know more about this woman. Then, she heard the Elder saying, "Granddaughter, I am speaking to you!"

"I'm sorry, Grandfather. I am listening."

"My wife has not been far away during the time we have spent together. She has been a great help to me in teaching you. Now she tells me you are ready."

Ready for what, Annie had no idea. But she remained silent, and let him continue. "Your blood does not run full of Indian blood—only a portion of it —but your heart and mind do. Being a full blood does not necessarily make you an Indian. It is what's here, in your heart and spirit, that makes you an Indian. So many of our young ones all across our lands have denounced their heritage and taken up the ways of the white world. Now some are slowly finding their way back, and this makes our hearts glad. You would not dishonor your ancestors, but you also reached a time in your life when you knew you must seek out and learn the way of your other side. You did not come to us on your own, so do not take credit for it. You were brought here by forces stronger than yourself. You have listened and learned well. You have much yet to learn, but now, it is up to you. I will tell you this; you must keep your heart true to your newfound path. As you already know, others will try to pull you away from your path. They will tell you that the way you have chosen no longer works in this technical world. But, you and I know where the truth really lies, and sooner or later, they too will know.

"Women, I'm proud to say, were given great power by our Creator. Over times past, the power of a woman has been buried. Men in other cultures convinced their women that they were of lesser value. This is not so in the Cherokee culture. We hold our women in high esteem. After all, they are the life-givers and they have always had a say in what happens to their sons and daughters, and in their way of life. Men and women are different, but they each hold wisdom in their own right. Joining that wisdom together makes for a strong people. Burying one or the other only weakens a people."

Their tea had cooled enough to drink, and they sat in

silence, enjoying the sweet, soothing drink. As a child, Annie had not been fond of sassafras tea, but she found this tea, sweetened with honey, to be very good. Annie commented on the delightful flavor of the tea, and the old woman lowered her eyes, saying "Thank you. I'm glad you enjoy it. I will teach you how to brew it, if you like."

Her English was a little broken, and Annie knew the old woman was more comfortable speaking her own language, so Annie addressed the Elder with a question. "Why are you telling me this, Grandfather? Sometime back, we discussed the roles of men and women."

"Yes, I know," he said, "but now you, as do many women your age and older, have an obligation to help guide younger women to an understanding of the power that is lying asleep within them. Teach them how to once again join in the circle. Teach them to do the circle dance so our world can be whole again and in balance. Do not demand to be heard, but teach those who have not heard how to listen with open minds and hearts. Do you understand?"

"Yes, Grandfather, but how am I to do this?"

"Do not worry about it. You will be shown the way," he said, simply with smile.

"Now for your gift." The Elder nodded his head toward his wife, and continued, "This woman, who is far wiser to the ways of women than I, tells me you have earned the right to be given a new name."

Annie was stunned; she had never heard of this custom.

"This name," he said, "you will not use in your everyday life. To do so would dishonor your parents for the name you received at your birth. You may, if you so choose, share it with others close to you. But the Ancients will now know you by this name. When you wish to call upon them, use this name, and they will hear."

He looked at his wife, and she spoke in almost a whisper. "You will now be know to us as *'Woman Who Walks Alone.'*"

Pleasure washed over Annie! Yes, the name fit her well, and she would carry it with pride. The old couple could see Annie's joy by the smile on her face. They sat quietly for a while, letting Annie absorb this great moment.

Finally, Annie was able to speak. "I am honored," she said. "This is a most unexpected gift, and I thank you both. I feel you have chosen well."

They both laughed. "Oh! We did not choose," the Elder said, still laughing. "The name was given to us to give to you. We are only the messengers."

"I see," Annie said, and, as she started to open her mouth for a question, the Elder gave her that look--the look that told her not to question.

CHAPTER 11

WE CALLED YOU TO THE MOUNTAIN. WHY DID YOU NOT COME?

—*The Hawks*

When Spring arrived in full bloom, the Elder also seemed to bloom. He grew stronger, and the glow returned to his face. This made Annie's heart as light as the breezes that blew up the river valley. She thanked God for hearing her prayer that he not be taken from this earth.

It was time for Annie to start planning her garden. On a day when the sun shone warm and the skies were clear, Annie decided to cut down some brush around the perimeter of her garden. Because of the warmth, she proceeded without her heavy work gloves. After about an hour of work, Annie had a strong feeling that she was being called to the mountain. She had never ignored the calling, but she wanted so badly to get this chore completed, she kept telling herself, "Later. Later, I will go."

In the next moment, as Annie reached down to remove a small bush, she felt a slight prick in her left thumb. It felt like a small sticker, but when she looked down, she saw a large purple thorn penetrating her knuckle and protruding from the other side. There was no pain, so Annie did not worry about it. She returned to the cabin and extracted the thorn with a pair of tweezers, taking care not to break it off. Still, there was no pain. Annie poured antiseptic into the small wound and returned to her work. She went directly to the spot where she had encountered the thorn, and looked for the bush, with perhaps a little revenge in her heart. Despite searching everywhere in the general area, Annie could find no such bush. Where was it?

"I know it was right here!" she told herself. "I must be losing my mind! Oh, well, no real harm done," she reasoned, returning to the job at hand. Since this was the only area around her cabin that received sunlight, the brush would shade her garden. It had to go.

Without giving her wound another thought, Annie worked a few hours more. Soon, however, she grew tired, and the sun on her back burned hot. Then, she became cold with chills, and then, again, hot and lightheaded. "What is wrong with me?" Annie wondered. She had always been healthy as a horse, rarely sick. "Maybe I've had enough work for today," she thought, and decided to go to the cabin to rest. When she drew her hands from the dense undergrowth, she saw that her thumb had swollen to double its normal size and had turned purple. The discoloration and swelling was spreading to the rest of her hand, but still, Annie felt no pain. By the time she made it to her cabin, it took all of her remaining strength to climb the stairs to the porch. She felt as weak as a newborn foal. Feeling hot and cold at the same time, she realized she was ill...unlike anything she had experienced before.

    Half walking, half crawling, she made it to the couch in the front room of the cabin. She knew she needed to use ice on her hand, but decided to rest a few minutes, then to try to make it to the kitchen. As she lay, drifting in and out of consciousness, her mind seemed muddled, and she couldn't hold a clear thought. Fear started to creep up her spine, but Annie was aware enough to resist it. Now, she felt pain -- a throbbing, intense pain that surrounded her hand and was shooting up her arm! Annie had received medical training in her younger days, and knew what she should do, but was unable to do anything. Using all of her remaining strength, she lifted her left arm with her right hand and raised the injured one above her head, thinking it might help. The pain subsided somewhat, and Annie drifted into a deep sleep. Visions came to her sleeping mind. In a vision, she stood in her garden, while three hawks circled above. Their eyes red with anger, they said, "We called you to the mountain. Why did you not come?" Annie shook with fear and sank to her knees. Then the hawks departed, flying back toward the mountain. Annie tried to get up and follow, but her legs would not function. Everything went black. How long she slept, Annie had no idea, but when she awoke, it was dark outside and she was cold. The pain had returned. The skin, stretched and hot, around her wound throbbed with the swelling, but her mind had cleared enough for Annie to realize she had to do something to help herself. Her kitchen lay only a few feet from her, but as she made her way across the floor, supporting herself on furniture, the distance of a few feet grew to be miles.

    She did not remember wrapping ice in a towel or going

back to the couch, but when she awoke a second time, the ice had melted and her dogs were whining and nudging her. Annie felt a little stronger now. She realized that neither she nor her animals had been fed in a long time. Feeding the animals required every ounce of her energy, so she fed them and returned immediately to the couch and her covers.

The next day, Annie's fever was still high, and food would not pass her lips. She knew she needed nourishment, but even when she could get food down, it would not stay down. For seven days, Annie's illness raged. Caring for her animals was all she could accomplish. On the sixth day, her fever broke, and that night, she was able to keep down the broth she drank. The wound's swelling had subsided, but the knuckle of her thumb refused to bend for several months.

When she was able to get out again, Annie returned to the place where the offending bush should have been. It was not there. Moreover, a bush with that type of thorn was nowhere to be found in the woods around her cabin.

In another week, Annie had regained her strength. When she felt confident that she could drive safely, she went to see the Elder. He and his wife greeted her with a smile and addressed her by her new name. The old woman retreated to the kitchen, and Annie sat down across from the Elder. He studied her face for a while, and then said, "You have been ill, Granddaughter." It was not a question, but a statement.

"Yes, Grandfather. I had a strange illness." She told him of the events leading to her sickness, of the sickness itself, and of her recovery.

The Elder sat in silence for a long time, then spoke to her, "Do you understand what happened?"

Without hesitation, Annie answered, "Yes, Grandfather. I didn't go to the mountain when I was called...so I suffered."

"Granddaughter, did you at any time feel death coming

for you?" he asked, and leaned forward for her answer.

"No," Annie said, "but the pain and illness were quite enough."

"Well," he said, "the ancients were not really punishing you. They were only getting your attention."

"I'll say they did!" was Annie's reply. "Now I know better. When I'm called to the mountain, short of having a broken back, I had better go!"

The Elder smiled warmly, saying, "I'm sorry you had to go through what you did. Now, let's have some tea and speak of more pleasant things." And as he spoke, his wife entered the room, carrying three cups of her wonderful sassafras tea.

CHAPTER 12

WHY SHOULD THE MOTHER MAKE IT EASY FOR YOU TO GATHER HER BOUNTY?

—*The Elder*

On her drive home that evening, Annie made plans for the work ahead of her. The last frost had laid its silvery blanket across the land. Old Cold Maker had loosened his grip. It was time for Annie to plant her garden. Working the soil manifested the hardest part of this task. It was at this time of year that her farmer-grandfather would return to her. Although she could not actually see him, she could feel his presence, smiling and guiding her as she prepared the earth to accept the seeds. Her grandfather had been so good at this, and had passed on to her some of his skill. Once satisfied with the mix of soil and fertilizer, she made holes with her hoe, spacing them equally, and placing three seeds in each hole. She never planted two seeds, and never four, but always three in each hole...her sacred number. As she covered the seeds, she asked for the Earth Mother's blessings.

Spring held only kindness that year. The seeds sprang forth and grew well. Water, sun, and good soil were truly the essences of life! Spring also brought fish back to the river, after their long winter in deep holes of the many river-fed lakes. Annie spent a few evenings each week fishing and relaxing on the river bank. She made an offering of tobacco to the water, then cast her line, and waited. Sometimes she caught nothing, but when she caught fish, she thanked each one for its life. Annie kept only those she needed, releasing the rest. A couple of fish, a few times each week, were all she needed. Occasionally, Annie kept a few extra fish to take to the Elder and his wife. They accepted them with great pleasure, and, as the old woman prepared them for supper, the Elder would tell Annie fish stories from the old days.

"At one time," he would say, "fish were plentiful in all the streams, rivers, and lakes. They were so plentiful that even the smallest of children could help catch fish for their families. In the fall, the people would dry and smoke the fish to be stored for the winter when fish would again be hard to find. Still, they took only as much as they needed." He would then explain, in detail, how the people preserved the fish.

Annie enjoyed hearing the Elder speak of the old ways. He seemed to enjoy telling the stories as much as Annie enjoyed hearing them. His eyes would sparkle as he reminisced about his youth.

Even though Annie was no longer formally his student, she never came away from the Elder's cabin without some new knowledge. In his own way, the Elder made sure that Annie continued to learn, and Annie thirstily drank in the new knowledge. In her younger days, she had hated school. It had bored her, making it a struggle to get passing grades. But now, Annie could not get enough of the Elder's wisdom and teachings. She would spend at least one full afternoon a week with him and his wife. Annie so looked forward to her visits that she rushed through her chores to make sure she had plenty of time with the Elder.

Summer gave goodness to the land, as well as to Annie. More food grew in her garden than she could use. Of course, her gifts for the Elder were gifts of food throughout the season. Knowing his fondness for tomatoes and cucumbers, Annie cultivated a few extra plants just for him. The Elder and his wife grew a small patch of corn (or, "maize"), which they shared with Annie when the harvest was good. It was the best corn she had ever tasted. When Annie asked for the Elder's secret to growing such delicious corn, he smiled and answered, "Respect."

Annie roamed the woods and coves that summer, as she had done every summer since her arrival in the mountains. She gathered berries, roots, wild onions, and garlic, which she would dry, can, or make into jams and jellies. Wild strawberries were her favorite, but, because they were so small, it took days to gather enough for a batch of jam. The Elder laughed at her whenever she showed up at his cabin with her fingers stained red and purple, complaining that the sweetest wild fruit seemed to be the smallest and most difficult to gather.

"Well," he would say, "why should the Mother make it easy for you to gather her bounty? When the fruit is difficult to gather, you do not take every last one. You leave some for her other children...the animals and the birds. I'm sure you never forget to leave an offering when you take from the berry patch or dig a root."

No, Annie never forgot. To forget to leave an offering

would show disrespect to the Mother, and Annie determined she would not risk doing anything in her new found way of life to anger the Mother. She needed all the help she could get.

CHAPTER 13

WE MUST FIND A WAY TO STOP THE WORLDS' BLOODSHED. THE ANSWER IS HELD BY THOSE COMING AFTER US.
—The Elder

Annie worked most of the day weeding her garden, and wondered why the weeds grew so much better than the vegetables. She finished with enough daylight to go fishing. Since she had only one fish left in the freezer, she needed to ask the river for a few more. Annie loved the old river, anyway, and any excuse to go there brought her joy. She had learned that the Indians called this river "Long Man," though it had since been renamed, "The Little Tennessee." This river rambled for miles before joining the Tennessee River.

Annie could sit for hours, letting the river talk to her. It had seen so much and knew so much. It told her of the laughter and tears that were mixed within its waters. She often thought of the Cherokee who had lived on the river's banks. Were they happy here? Did they know peace as she did? Yes, she concluded; they must have known peace on this river until they were driven away in the Trail of Tears.

When she sat quietly on this riverbank, she felt the spirits of those who had been here before her. Long Man also held secrets that he would not give away. Like the earth, the water also holds memories. Although there were places here where Annie felt at peace, there were also places here where she felt pain, confusion and fear. She soon learned from her ancient memories that in these places, where pain and fear swept into her soul, blood, tears, and death had been spilled. Whenever Annie reflected on this, she, too, released her tears to join Long Man and Mother Earth.

She always asked the same question, "Why must mankind bury the souls and spirits of others to fulfill their own desire for power and greed?" Annie felt no one had the answer, for it continues to happen all over the world. Many times, Annie brought this question to the Elder. Even he had no answer for her.

She asked him once if he held animosity toward the white race for the pain they had caused the ancestors. He had said, "No, what is done is done, and anger is a waste of emotional energy." Adding, "We must find a way to stop the world's bloodshed. The answer is held by those coming after us. Teaching hatred for one group or another will come back against those who hate and teach hate."

The Elder had looked deep into Annie's eyes and added, "Never forget the circle."

Annie had a hot temper, and throughout her life, she had to constantly keep it in check. She had so often wanted to lash out at others or at herself when something went wrong.

Now, when these feelings arose in her, the Elder's teaching to just be would come to mind. She knew that this teaching did not mean she should let others run her life, nor did it mean she should allow others to pull her away from her beliefs. She knew that she would still fight for herself and her rights, and for the rights of those who could not fight for themselves. Annie's way had become a quiet way, and she was still learning.

The Elder knew these things about Annie, though Annie wasn't sure how he knew. He would tease her about being a 'silent hunter.' Then he would chuckle and say, "Silent hunters should be feared more than screaming, thundering ones, even in the animal kingdom. But then, you already knew that. There are people who have something to say, and then there are those who just have to say something. The latter feel they must impress others with how much they know or how much they think they know. Those who talk all the time never hear. Wisdom cannot be built this way.

"Annie, you talk very little these days, except when you are full of questions," he once said with a smile. "Do not be afraid to share with others what you have learned, if they ask. That is an obligation we must honor if we are to help the young ones. Those who are boastful are never really heard. Stay humble, and you will reach the young when your time is right. The ancients will know that time, and will help guide you.

"There are men and women who have been entrusted with the oral history and knowledge of the people. They are known as the 'Wisdom Keepers.' Not only do they know of the physical world, but they also know of the spiritual world. The Wisdom Keepers are given the gift of retaining this knowledge, so they can pass it on to the next generation, which will then, in turn, pass it on to the next."

He rose from his rocker, and, as Annie had seen him do many times, walked to the window and gazed lovingly upon the mountains. After a long silence, he spoke again as if explaining to someone in the mountains, "I am not a Wisdom Keeper. I am considered a teacher for my people and I am honored to pass on what I have learned during my long earth walk. Long ago, I was the student. In my mind's eye, I can still see my teacher and feel fondness for him. He was my uncle, the brother of my mother. It was our people's custom to have a boy's uncle teach him, if his mother had a brother. In my case, this uncle was a very good and compassionate teacher."

He had turned to face Annie, with a bit of sadness in his eyes, saying, "You and I were brought together for a reason. You were seeking truths and knowledge. I hope I have been of some help in your quest. If I have guided you to the path for which you were searching, then I have fulfilled my duty and can go to my next life with a peaceful heart. However, it does not end here, as we have discussed before. You, along with the others who have come to me, are to pass on to others what you have learned. You have been given a gift, as I was given. Share this gift, because gifts hold no value unless they are given to others."

Hearing this, Annie had felt her blood turn cold. The Elder stood there, preparing her for a time when he would no longer be here. She did not want to think about that, for she was not ready to let him go. "Would he see another winter?" In her heart, she felt he knew he would not. Sadness had begun to creep into her. "No," she had vowed to herself. "I will mourn for him, but I will honor him by doing as he has requested. In this way, he will live on."

A tear had run down her cheek, then, as softly as a feather's touch, the Elder had brushed away the tear. Waving his hand, he had said, "Go, now child. I have work to do."

The memory of that day faded, and Annie returned to the present, struggling to remember what she had been doing before losing herself in her memories. "Oh, yes," she reminded herself, "I was going fishing!"

Resuming her walk to the river, fishing rod in hand, the memory of that day with the Elder resurfaced. She understood what the Elder had expected of her, but she did not yet know how she was to do it. The Elder had said that the ancients would guide her, so for now, Annie decided to attend to the river and her fishing. As she was settling down and checking out her old rod and reel, she saw the man she had often seen before, fishing on the other side of the river. She waved and smiled; he did likewise. Annie had never met this man, nor spoken to him. At this wide stretch of river, words could not be heard over the roar of the water, but Annie could see the friendly man and that he enjoyed the sport of fishing.

Annie never started her fishing expedition by immediately wetting her line. Instead, she would sit quietly for a while, just watching the river flow past her. On this day, she saw the man's rod bend, and he began slowly reeling in his catch. Gently, he retrieved the fish from the water. Just as gently, he removed the hook, then returned the fish to the river, with a look of reverence. The fish had been a fair-sized, smallmouth bass. Now that she thought about it, Annie had never seen the man keep a fish. Perhaps he just liked to fish, but did not care to eat his catch. The man's success was a good sign to her that the fish were biting.

Annie made her offering on the water and humbly asked for a fish or two to give themselves to her. She cast her line and waited...and waited...and waited...with not so much as a nibble. It would soon be dark and she would have to give up for the day, so she cast her eyes to the heavens and pleaded,

"Please God, send me just one fish."

Just then, from the corner of her eye, she saw a large bird flying down river toward her. As the bird drew closer, she saw it held a fish in its talons. "Well, he got his dinner," she thought to herself. Then, just before he passed overhead, his talons opened and the fish dropped close to Annie. She could not believe her eyes! She began to laugh so hard that tears rolled down her face.

Retrieving the large, gold fish, she saw it was a carp--not a choice edible fish unless you're starving to death. Not quite that hungry, Annie thanked the bird and the river anyway. She left the dead fish where it had fallen, thinking the bird might come back for it. If not, the raccoons would have a good meal.

Feeling a little embarrassed, she glanced across the river to see if the man had witnessed the scene that had just taken place. He had vanished. It struck her as strange that he had been there just before she spotted the bird, but was now gone. Could he be . . .? No, he was real, she knew. Still, it puzzled her that he seemed to always be on the other side of the river whenever she came, and she never saw him come or go. It would be another question for the Elder, if she dared!

CHAPTER 14

MY HEART STOPPED BEATING FOR A SECOND AND AIR WOULD NOT GO INTO MY LUNGS. TEARS FILLED MY EYES, AND I WEPT OUT OF CONTROL.

—Annie

August arrived with much warmer weather than is considered normal in the mountains. The river became a place of gathering for the people who live there and for those who were visiting. The water of the Little Tennessee stayed cold and refreshing throughout the summer. Annie's mother had said that Annie had been a water baby. True to her mother's description, Annie swam as comfortably as she roamed the woods or climbed the mountainside. She often took her dogs to the river, where they would play for hours in the cool, clear water.

August passed into September, and the heat continued.

Annie grew restless for the first time since her arrival in the mountains. Having so many people around kept her on edge. She understood the others had as much right to be there as did she, but it annoyed her that they always wanted to talk. They asked her questions about the area, as though word had gotten out that, in her short time here, she had been intent on learning all she could about the land and its history.

Someone once mentioned to her that she should make some money being a tour guide of the back country, but that was the last thing Annie wanted to do! There were many sacred places in these mountains, and Annie would have no part in bringing people to these places who would not understand nor show proper respect for the Great Mother. The sacred places where not meant to be playgrounds for tourists.

Annie had found many of the sacred places on her own or through the guidance of the ancients. The Elder had told her of some of the places. When she visited these mountains or valleys, she would sometimes feel almost non-human. Her animal instincts would become strong and comforting. With each visit, she offered up prayers and left an offering to thank the animal spirits; still, many secrets would never be shared, and this was as it should be.

Annie had learned from the ancients that these mountains were the oldest in the world. At one time, they were higher than any mountains known to modern man. To release all of their memories would bring devastation to them. Although mankind would always try to unravel the mysteries of Mother Earth, it would never be done, according to the ancients. From time to time, some secrets would be released; never all, for this is part of the circle.

One day, when Annie yearned to escape humanity, she returned to what she now called "Wolf Mountain." Remembering what the Elder had told her about its mysteries and powers, she walked softly in moccasined feet. She felt that if she did speak, she should do so in a whisper, as if she were in a church. She followed the same trail she had followed when she had come to this mountain before. In her heart, Annie wished she would once again encounter the wolf, but she knew she would not.

Reaching the bald, where, on her previous trip, she had eaten her lunch and seen the deer; she sat down to nibble on a piece of jerky and drink water from her canteen. Annie watched the woods below her. Suddenly, she heard a slight rustling in the bush behind her. Turning slowly, she saw a woman, standing maybe fifty feet away, holding a strange looking stick. The woman looked a bit older than Annie, but was not yet what Annie would call "old." Annie glanced around to see if any others were near, but saw only the woman. The woman walked toward her, so Annie stood slowly, not sure what she should do. Annie's eyes were fixed upon the woman's face. She wanted to say something, but no sound would come from her mouth. Fear did not keep her from speaking, but a sense of awe and surprise. When the woman reached her, she said, "Si yu," the Cherokee word for "Hello." Annie, in turn, repeated the word, having learned its meaning, along with other Cherokee words, from the Elder. A smile crossed both of their faces. The woman then spoke in broken English. Her voice, deep and soft, soothed the perplexed Annie.

"I am sorry if I startled you," the woman said.

"No," Annie replied, "I was just surprised to see anyone else on the mountain."

Still smiling, the woman continued, "I come here often to offer prayers and to dig roots." The woman looked down at her digging stick, which was made of wood and worn very smooth where hands had handled it for a very long time. The digging end was shaped like a narrow "V," somewhat like a spade; but it had been carved as one continuous piece, which was now also worn smooth.

Annie motioned for the woman to sit down, as she offered her a piece of jerky and some water. The woman accepted, saying "Wa do" (Thank you). From a leather bag which was tied around her waist, the woman then drew out corn cakes, wrapped in cloth, which she held out to Annie. Accepting a cake, Annie repeated, "Wa do." They sat quietly for a while, enjoying the jerky, cakes and water. Annie felt comfortable and content, as if she were in the presence of an old friend.

After they finished the food, Annie waited for the woman to open the conversation. Finally, the woman asked, "What are you called?"

"My English name is Annie."

The woman then asked, "Do you carry the blood of the people?"

"Yes," Annie said, "from my mother."

"Were you born in the land of the people?" the woman asked.

"No," Annie replied, "I was born to the north of here on a farm."

The woman started to speak again, but stopped herself. Then, after a moment of thought, during which she never took her eyes off Annie's face, she said, "I am again sorry. I should not be asking so many questions. It is not proper."

Annie, indeed, had begun to wonder why this woman seemed so interested in someone she had just met, when the woman spoke again. "I make no excuses for my rudeness," she said, "only to say that a memory came forward in my mind, of a woman my great grandmother spoke of when I was a child." She then began to relate a story.

"The woman was young, beautiful, and always happy. Everyone liked and respected her. She belonged to the Deer Clan. My great grandmother was also of the Deer Clan, and as children, these two friends were inseparable. They were like sisters. As they grew older, but before they reached womanhood, this girl would disappear for long periods of time. No one knew where she was, and her mother and brothers would search the village and the surrounding woods, never finding a sign of her. When she would finally return, around dark, her mother would ask her where she had been. She would only say that she was with her friends on the mountain. More and more, she would tell her mother the same story of where she had been.

"Then, one night, she returned home long after dark. As she entered the cabin, the entire family turned to stare at her, as if they were a little frightened. She had a wildness about her that they had never seen. She also carried a musky odor. Her father was very angry with her. He forbid her to leave the village except to tend the crops. Since children in those days, never disobeyed their parents, she did as she was told, but she never laughed or played again. It was like her spirit had died.

"When she was of the age to take a husband, she chose a white man. He was a trader who came often to the village. My great grandmother said that she knew her friend did not marry the white man for love, but had done so to spite her father. Not much time passed before she bore this man a son, then another, then another. Though having one child right after another is usually very hard on a woman, those babies put a bit of sparkle back in this woman's eyes.

"The rest of her life was very difficult. Her husband, a heavy drinker of strong spirits, almost daily raised his voice and hand to her. She endured for the sake of her sons. The only time she knew any peace was when her husband went away on a trading trip. Since their cabin was not far from the village, my great grandmother had remained her friend, and had gone to visit her often when she knew that the white husband was away. Many times, she begged her friend to leave this man and return to the village and her people. She promised that the people would care for her and for her sons, and she would no longer have to live in fear, but her friend refused.

"Everyone knew that her husband had other women in the towns where he traded. Maybe that was the reason she would not return to her family; she had fear of bringing shame on the tribe. Most of the village had stopped trading with her husband, and, in her mind, she too was an outcast for making such a poor choice.

"It was forbidden in the Cherokee culture for a man to ever strike his wife or his children. If he did, he was banished from the tribe forever.

"Early one morning, when frost covered the ground, the woman came limping into the village, assisted by her sons, who were now young men. She looked much older then her years. Blood had dried around her mouth, and her eyes were swollen half shut. She had been beaten badly, and she did not seem to know where she was. When my great grandmother saw them coming up the trail, she ran to help. Looking into the eyes of the woman's sons, she saw both pleading and rage. My great grandmother didn't have to ask what had happened; she knew.

"When they had taken their mother inside where the women could care for her, the woman's sons went back outside. The young men explained that they had been away on a hunting trip for two days, and on the morning of their return, they found their mother lying on the floor of the cabin. They had two choices: to take their mother to her people for help, or go after their father. They decided to deal with their father later."

Annie's companion stopped speaking and reached for the canteen. Annie then asked, "And did they deal with their father?"

The woman stopped drinking, swallowed, and said, "No one knows for sure, but he was never seen again; not even in the towns of other villages where he traded. In time, the broken woman healed physically, and even her spirit seemed to return to her, but she was never the same. She spoke little, and whenever she was able, she would roam the woods as if looking for something.

"On a day in early spring, the woman called her sons to her. They were now into their manhood and could care for themselves. What was said in her small dwelling, no one ever knew, but the following day, she emerged with a basket of belongings and walked off into the mountains, never to return to the people. From time to time, women out gathering berries, herbs or roots, would catch a glimpse of her. She always stopped, turned, and smiled, then would move quietly into the woods like an animal. The name she had carried all of her life was never spoken again. The Elders of the tribe gave her a new name."

The woman stopped talking to take another drink of water, giving Annie the opportunity to ask, "What was her new name?"

The woman put the canteen down slowly, and rose as if to leave. Annie also rose, fearing she had asked the wrong question. Then, looking deep into Annie's eyes--or past them into her very soul, the woman said, "You do not know?"

"No," Annie said, "How could I know?"

Then, the woman smiled with the warmth of an angel and said softly, "She was then known as 'Woman Who Walks

Alone.'" She then turned and walked away, not looking back.

For a split second, Annie's heart stopped beating, and air would not go into her lungs. Tears filled her eyes, and she began shaking until her legs would no longer hold her. The surprised woman, overcome with shock, sank to the ground and wept, out of control.

CHAPTER 15

YOU HAVE SEEN AND HEARD ONE OF YOUR PASSED LIVES. IT HAS BEEN GIVEN AS A GIFT; CARRY IT GENTLY IN YOUR HEART.
—The Elder

Darkness roamed the mountain as Annie descended the rugged terrain and drove home. She remembered little of the trip, traveling as though she were in a fog. Upon reaching her cabin, she, and her dogs and cats, did not greet each other as they usually did. They seemed to know something about her had changed. Annie completed her evening chores of feeding her animals, cleaning up her cabin, and building a fire. She accomplished all this in silence, moving like a robot. She could not get her mind past the woman on the mountain nor the story the woman had told. Annie stood under a hot shower for a long time, trying to find her way back to reality. A thought flashed into her mind that her encounter on the mountain had just been a dream, but she knew better when she found two corn cakes, given to her by the stranger, in her day pack.

When Annie crawled into her bed around midnight, she collapsed, overtaken by total exhaustion. Even so, sleep would not bless her. Her mind visioned the image of the woman in the story, and tears began falling onto her pillow. How could she feel so close to a woman who had lived over a hundred years ago? Another question came into her mind. Should she speak to the Elder about this? He was her mentor, and had guided her through other strange happenings. She would consider it for a few days, then decide. For now, she just wanted to escape from the world into sleep, but this was not to be.

Rising from her bed, she wrapped herself in a blanket and walked onto the porch. The night had turned cold and clear. Annie studied the stars, finding The Three Sisters. She asked, "Ancient Ones, why have you given me this puzzle? What do you wish for me to find?" No answer came to her mind. Annie sat there the rest of the night. Her feet were bare and the blanket she had wrapped around herself had not kept out the cold, but her mind was not registering her physical discomfort.

With the morning's first light, Annie finally went back inside, built up the fire, dressed herself, and made a cup of strong coffee. She had to release this or find answers, and she felt that neither would be easy. After drinking her coffee, she decided to go to the mountain beside her cabin. This place always brought her a sense of peace and balance.

Pulling on her knee-high moccasins, and taking only her canteen of water and walking stick, she began to climb with her dogs at her heels. At the top, she offered up a prayer and made an offering of tobacco to the mountain spirits. She then sat down in a cross-legged position and let her mind go, reaching for that deep, dark void of meditation. Before long, visions began entering her mind's eye. She saw a woman standing on a mountain bald. Warm wind blew her long, black hair away from her face, and she was smiling. She was young and very beautiful. Soon, the woman spoke in a musical voice, saying, "Friends, I have come to play! where are you?" As if by magic, animals of all kinds came into view from the surrounding woods. There appeared bears, deer, raccoons, wolves, beaver, and other fur bearers. Above her, hawks, owls, ravens, red birds and blue birds lit in the trees. Turkeys and grouse pecked around the young woman's feet. She spoke to each one of the them, stroking their fur or feathers. Then, she began to sing, and each creature began to dance in a circle. The young woman joined the circle.

Soon, the dancing stopped, and yet the young woman played. They played hide and seek and tag. The entire mountain was alive! Even the trees seemed to be smiling and swaying. Sun Boy had marched to his western home and the red glow in the sky behind this scene made it very eerie, yet beautiful. Then, with no words nor signal that Annie could hear or see, the activity stopped. The animals retreated back into the woods and the woman again stood alone. She faced the setting sun, raised her arms, and spoke in Cherokee. Annie could not hear her soft words well enough to make out what was being said, but she guessed it was the young woman's evening prayer. Upon finishing her prayer, the young woman turned and started back down the trail. Annie called for her to wait, but, of course, the woman did not hear her. Annie's mind slowly left the dark void and the vision was carried away.

Annie looked around, watching, now, the setting sun of this world. There was no question in Annie's mind who this woman was. And she had seen the friends with whom the young woman played on the mountain. Well, at least some part of the mysterious story had been shown to Annie. But, why had all of this come to Annie, and who was the woman with whom she had shared jerky and corn cakes? Would she ever see her again? Annie decided to present the mystery to the Elder. She now concluded that she was not wise enough to figure it out--or maybe she was just impatient.

The following morning, as Annie drove to the Elder's cabin, a cold fall rain began to beat against her windshield. The night before, she had put a small load of wood into the bed of her truck to take to the Elder. Oh, well, wet wood was better than no wood, and it would dry out under his overhanging porch.

After Annie entered the Elder's cabin and went through all of the formalities, she asked him to help her with a mystery. She had decided not to put it to him as a question, knowing that he grew weary of questions, and had been urging her to learn from her ancient memories. But this mystery seemed to exist behind a locked door that she could not open alone. The Elder agreed to help her, and she told him everything. He listened intently, and did not interrupt, until she fell silent and looked at him with questioning eyes.

Rising from his rocker, he said, "Come. Let's sit on the porch so we can enjoy the rain." He wrapped the blanket from his nephew around his shoulders and handed Annie another one. It was soft with age, and she felt as if she were one with it. They sat in two old rockers and gazed out at the misty mountains. It was not long before the Elder's wife came out with two steaming cups of hot apple cider, a cinnamon stick in each one. The old woman smiled her toothless smile and addressed Annie by the new name they had given her. The old woman saw Annie flinch a bit, but pretended not

Sleep With The Wolf—Walk With The Bear

to notice. As she turned to go back inside, Annie asked, "Grandmother, are you not going to join us?"

"Not today," she said in her broken English, "this old man of mine has torn yet another shirt and my mending is getting ahead of me." She padded away on her tiny feet.

Annie and the Elder sat quietly for a while, sipping the hot cider. When Annie could stand it no longer, she spoke in a tone an octave higher than normal. "Well, Grandfather, am I losing my mind, or is this a mystery I am unable to unravel?"

He spoke without taking his eyes from the mountains, "It is so simple--you cannot see the forest for the trees, as the saying goes."

"Grandfather, I do not see it as simple; but then, I am not as wise as you are." She said, knowing she must remain respectful, even though she became suspicious that he was making fun of her.

"I believe," he continued, "the English word for it is 'reincarnation.' We have discussed this belief before, have we not?"

"Yes, Grandfather," Annie said, "but how?"

He stopped her in mid-sentence, saying, "Drink your cider. Look at the mist on the mountains. Quiet your mind. I'm sure you will then see."

Annie did as she was told, concentrating on quieting her mind. She heard nothing but the rain. She watched the mist, which now seemed to be swirling and moving about. The face of the young woman appeared to Annie. From her mind to Annie's, a message was delivered, "My physical form has returned only long enough for me to find the one who now carries my spirit. I am not disappointed; you are a seeker of truth. Of course, it seems to have taken a long time to find your way here, but I understand that the time was not right until now. I also returned to find you, so I could tell you that I am sorry you had to be born with some of the sadness and pain I endured during my walk. Since you were given the strength of your mother, you have been able to withstand it well. Falling by the wayside from time to time is nothing to be ashamed of."

Annie knew what she meant, and nodded in agreement. The face faded and mist once again swirled. Annie now realized tears had been rolling down her cheeks, and the blanket across her breasts was wet. The Elder's eyes and Annie's met. He spoke softly. "You have seen and heard one of your past lives. It was given as a gift. Carry it gently in your heart. Protect it, for when your earth walk is complete, it will be passed to someone not yet born. Now, Granddaughter, do you understand from where your new name came?"

Annie could not speak; she only nodded her head, rose from the rocker, and walked into the rain toward the woods. She needed to be alone.

CHAPTER 16

*I DO SEE SOMETHING IN YOU, PERHAPS YOU, YOURSELF,
DO NOT SEE. I SEE YOU AS...*
—The Grandmother

That fall, the days danced around each other, wet and cold. The weather affected Annie's mood; restless all the time, with moments of depression. Her daily chores proved to be more difficult to complete. Something was just not right. Even when she went to the mountain, she could not find balance or peace. She sought out solitude, for even time with the Elder did not fulfill her.

In this difficult season, Annie found herself picking up book after book, staring at the words, not comprehending them. This was not like her at all! No matter what happened in her life, she usually told herself, "This too shall pass." But this strange feeling refused to pass, wrapping her in anger.

She had said nothing about this to the Elder, nor had she spoken of it to anyone else. Others had suffered with this emotion; her feelings were not unique.

There were days when she wanted to just run--to run so far and so hard that her lungs would burst. The depression would come and go with a blink of an eye...but the worst part became the restlessness. Annie skulked around her cabin like a caged animal. She had considered her cabin a beloved, safe haven from the outside world. Now, it became a prison. She knew the Elder could see that something bothered her, yet he did not pry. He had learned that when Annie needed to discuss something, she would open up to him sooner or later. Because she often said very little or nothing at all, the Elder called her "the silent hunter."

Finally, after about two months, Annie decided she could not deal with this on her own; she had already asked her guides to help her find the answers to her dilemma, to no avail. Had they abandoned her for reasons of which she was not aware? She went to see the Elder.

After the formalities, Annie spoke to him, almost pleading with him to help her before she did something rash. He said nothing to Annie, but called to his wife. When the old woman entered the room, the Elder turned to Annie and said, "This problem, I cannot help you with. This woman is the one who will guide you now."

Saying nothing, the old woman turned toward the door, beckoning Annie to follow. As they stepped outside, the old woman handed Annie her jacket, and took down a shawl for herself. Still, the woman said nothing, but turned and began walking up a path away from the cabin.

Stopping not far out of view of the cabin, the woman stopped and sat down on the dried grass. Annie did likewise. The old woman pulled her knees up to her chest and covered most of her small frame with her shawl. After she was satisfied with her position, she spoke in broken English, looking directly into Annie's eyes, "Tell me, if you wish, all that has been bothering you."

Annie nervously cleared her throat. This was the first time she and this woman had been alone together. She had come here looking for help. It was now offered from an unexpected source, but Annie proceeded.

As Annie explained what she had been feeling, the old woman did not interrupt, but simply nodded from time to time. After considerable thought, during which she was probably searching for the right English words, the old woman said, "I know that of which you speak. Not long after my first moon time (reaching womanhood) I encountered the woman which whom you shared food. I also heard a story of a woman who had walked the earth long before my birth. Of course, the story was quite different than the one you were given. At that time, there were few whites in our land, but tribes of different nations would war against one another, mostly over hunting grounds."

The old woman continued, speaking very slowly, as she struggled to find the English words. "The spirit within me was carried before by a young woman who had been killed during one of those raids. Her life gone before she married, she was never blessed with a child. Hearing this, I was made to understand why I would never bring forth life, something that saddened me deeply, but which I finally accepted. Also, because this woman died young, and tragically, her spirit within me became restless. I kept feeling as if I was supposed to be doing something, but I could not figure out what it was. Like you, I roamed the mountain tops a great deal, asking for guidance. This is when I met the woman on the mountain, much like you did."

The old woman then described the woman she met on the mountain. She described her appearance and the way she spoke--only, to this old woman, she spoke their native tongue.

The old woman continued, "I was what is called today a 'tomboy'. I did not want to do woman's work. I wanted to hunt and play the ball game. I wanted to do what the boys and men did, not tend crops, sew and cook. My mother said I would never become a wife if I did not learn these things, but at that time, I did not care. I wanted adventure! I dreamed of becoming a great warrior and leader. Of course, there was very little fighting going on then, except in Washington, over our lands.

"I'm sorry," the old woman suddenly said, "I am getting away from that of which we were speaking."

Annie shifted her position and said that was fine with her, for she had always wanted to know more about the Elder's quiet wife. The old woman laughed and said, "Oh, I am not always quiet; just ask that old man of mine!

"Now, where was I? Oh, yes, the woman on the mountain. I saw her and spoke with her many times."

Annie then asked, "Did she always have her digging stick with her?"

"Oh, yes," the old woman said, "and she had the best corn cakes I have ever tasted! How did you know about the digging stick?"

Annie explained what the stick looked like, and that she, too, had shared corn cakes with the woman on the mountain. They sat in silence for some time, both, no doubt, thinking the same thing.

No, Annie's mind objected, it could not have been the same woman; not in that long span of years! The one she met could have been the daughter of the woman known to the

Elder's wife. "Grandmother," she finally ventured, "you don't believe it was the same woman do you? It must have been her daughter!"

The old woman shrugged her shoulders, asking "Who is to say? The spirit world can be very hard to understand at times. However, the way you describe her, no two women, except twins perhaps, can look so much alike--not even a mother and daughter."

Annie grew silent again, then asked, "Did you know anything about her, like to what tribe she belonged, or where she lived, or whether she was married? Since she dug roots and gathered herbs, maybe she was a medicine woman?"

"This I did learn," said the old woman, "she was a medicine woman. She was of Cherokee blood, but she was never seen by any of my people. I know nothing more. However, as it turned out, she became my mentor and teacher. She helped me find out what I was supposed to do for my people. The more we talked, the more I found myself wanting to know about the herbs, plants and roots that had healing powers. This knowledge, she gave to me. I would meet with her often, but no one in my village knew she instructed me. I never knew why I was always to come alone, and never to tell anyone where I had been or what I had been doing. Over a long period of time, I gathered much knowledge of the healing powers that the Great Mother offers to mankind. I am sure you know the story about the plants, do you not?"

"Yes," Annie said, "but tell it to me again if you are not growing tired."

"I am not tired at all. I am enjoying our time together without menfolk around," she said with a smile, before continuing. "In our culture, as you know, mankind was brought here from another world, and was put upon the surface of the earth. Well, our kind grew swiftly and there became many of us. The animals, back then, could speak to one another much as we do today. Anyway, they became concerned about how humans were taking over the land, killing too many of their kind, and treading down the plants they fed on. They called a council and decided to inflict diseases upon humans--diseases that would help keep the humans under control. The plant world felt sorry for the people, so they too held council, and decided to ask the Creator to give some of the plants healing powers, so they could save the people and all other living things on Mother Earth. The Creator did as they asked and then taught certain members of each tribe how to use this gift. The gift was then passed down from one generation to the next. This is another part of the circle.

"As you know, it is not permitted to marry someone within your own clan. The old man, whom I had known since we were children, was of another clan. We were married well over seventy years ago.

"I was still being taught the ways of a healer and he the ways of a teacher, so our first few years together were not what you might call close. There was great love and respect, of course, but little time to share it. Over all of these years, we have respected and been proud of one another in what the other does. He never felt neglected when I was called, in the middle of the night, to care for one of the people. And I never felt neglected when he would spend so many hours with those who came to seek his wisdom. He says he is not a 'wisdom keeper,' but I see him as such a man."

Annie could hear great love in the old woman's voice when she spoke of her husband.

"We lived much closer to the main village then," explained the old woman. "We only left the reservation, or the town, now called Cherokee, when the young ones were giving up the old ways, and were permitting money and other things to control their lives. We could not stand to watch that happening to our people, so we came far into the mountains and built our cabin. Those who wish to learn the old ways come to us, and I'm happy to say more and more have come during the past few years."

Deep in thought, the old woman looked off into the surrounding mountains. Finally, she rose and said to Annie, "Come, let's walk for a while, and speak of your concerns, before my old bones freeze up."

Annie said nothing as she followed the old woman up the path. The path lay uneven and rocky from lack of use. The old woman took Annie's arm to balance herself. As they walked, she spoke, "Tell me...do you feel yourself a healer?"

"No!" Annie exclaimed.

"No, nor do I," said the old woman, "but I do see something else in you that perhaps you have not seen." The old woman continued to speak, never taking her eyes off the ground. "I see a balance in your mind; maybe not always toward yourself, but toward others. You are able to see their weaknesses and strengths. You have been taught how to open your mind to your ancient memories," she said.

As she spoke, the old woman observed Annie from the corner of her eye. "You do not permit yourself to use this skill often enough. You are not willing yet to put your trust in your ancient memories, maybe out of fear, maybe for other reasons. Is this not true?"

Annie was caught off guard. She had not expected the conversation to turn in this direction. Perplexed, she answered, "I don't know, Grandmother. All I know is that at times I feel confused, anxious, out of balance, and even angry, for no known reason. Restlessness is the worst feeling, though. My body and mind are turning against me as I grow older."

The old woman laughed at Annie's self blame. "Oh, my dear one," she said, "we all go through that! Don't blame it all on growing old. You are a cocoon, becoming a butterfly. This is not an easy journey, but you will fly free soon. Like I said before, I do not see you as a healer of the body, but I see you as a guide of the mind."

"A what of the what, Grandmother?" Annie blurted, incredulously.

"Never mind, you will learn soon enough. Return to the Mountain of the Wolf, as you call it; the woman will still be there. She will guide you as she did me. Don't be in such a hurry. This will ease your anxious feelings, at least. Now, help me back to the cabin. We have walked and talked enough for today."

CHAPTER 17

YOU ARE A STRONG AND BRAVE WARRIOR. YOU HAVE EARNED THE RIGHT TO LIVE AND FIGHT ANOTHER DAY. I HONOR YOU.
—Annie

Annie walked the old woman back to her cabin, and this time, Annie made the sassafras tea. They sat around the table in the warm kitchen and talked of other things: womanly things, mostly, and very pleasant ones. Annie found that the old woman had quite a sense of humor. The old woman taught her more of the Cherokee language, laughing whenever Annie became tongue-twisted and a word came out wrong. Annie knew that the laughter held only good fun, and she knew how beautifully the Cherokee language could flow when spoken correctly.

Annie had noticed that the Elder had gone when the two women returned from the woods. Not wanting to be nosy, but still curious, she asked where he might be. The old woman sipped her tea and said, "It will soon be sundown. I am sure he is out where he offers his evening prayers."

"Yes," Annie said, "it is sundown and I must be going. The day has slipped away so fast!" She stood and thanked the old woman for the afternoon and their talk.

The old woman smiled, saying, "We will talk again soon, after you have found some of the answers you are seeking. I will tell you again: do not force it. The answers will be given to you when the time is right." Then she laughed again, "Listen to me now. I sound like the old man!"

Annie drove home, feeling a little better, but something still nagged at her. She told herself that she would just have to stop worrying about it.

When she stepped onto her porch, she noticed a package that had been delivered while she was away. It was from her mother, who was always sending little things she thought Annie could use or would enjoy. Annie called them "care packages." Inside, she found a pair of warm gloves, some socks, a couple of sweaters, and some soft, fluffy towels. There was also a loving note, saying she hoped Annie could use the gifts, and that she looked forward to seeing her in the summer. Her mother knew that Annie could get these things for herself, but she was one of those people who enjoyed sending small gifts, without having a reason. Annie enjoyed receiving these touches of home. After emptying the care package and reading the note again, Annie resumed her evening chores. She fixed herself a bite to eat, then stepped into a hot shower. She realized then the tiredness she felt; more so mentally than physically. Annie's mind had been racing for days, and it all had finally caught up with her. Without even picking up her book to read, Annie fell into a deep sleep as soon as she lay down. This would be her first good night's sleep in a long time.

When Annie awoke, the sun peeked at her from over the

mountains. Her first thoughts were of the old woman and their conversation the day before. "Slow down," again came the advice of the old woman. "Keep your mind open, but do not expect so much so soon," she repeated to herself. Annie rose to add more wood to the fire, noticing that the nights were getting colder as fall progressed. Soon, winter would be upon them again. As she drank her morning coffee, feeling strong and rested, she also planned her day. Her first instinct was to return to Wolf Mountain in hopes of seeing the woman with a digging stick. A voice spoke inside her head, "There you go again, pushing for answers. Anyway, she won't be there today." Annie looked into her coffee cup, as if reading tea leaves. Such voices in her head no longer came as a surprise. She had grown used to them, and had found that, only when she did not follow their message, did she get herself into trouble.

"Okay, okay," Annie said aloud, as if speaking to someone in the room. "I have plenty to do around here anyway. Because of my lousy mood, I have neglected my fall chores to get ready for winter. Now, do I cut wood first, or gather nuts and fall roots?"

The thought of walking the riverbank for nuts sounded more appealing than cutting wood. She'd cut wood another day. The older Annie got, the more inviting became the idea of turning on a switch for heat. But that would cost money--something of which she had precious little.

Retrieving her baskets, she headed for the river. Long Man was running full due to fall rains. It made no difference whether the river was high or low; it welcomed her and put her at peace. She made a small offering at each tree. The nuts were releasing their grip to the mother tree and covering the ground. Because of this year's good rains, they were full. Squirrels scampered around, also gathering nuts for the winter. Annie spoke softly to them, as always, but they paid little attention to her.

With her gaze on the ground, Annie did not notice that she was approaching a small creek feeding the river. Suddenly, her dogs let out a low "woof" sound, and Annie looked up to see three deer, all doe's. As they stood looking at her, Annie sank to the ground and called her dogs to her. She knew the dogs were making the deer nervous. Somehow knowing they were safe, the deer returned to their drinking, then ambled away, with their thirst satisfied. Annie praised her dogs for not making a fuss, and for resisting running after the deer. Seeing wildlife always lightened Annie's heart.

"Yes," she thought to herself, "I'm going to be okay." Whatever had brought on her strange mood seemed to be lifting, at least for now. Annie's baskets were full, but she had brought along a cloth sack to gather a few extra nuts for the Elder and his wife. This brought the old woman once again to Annie's mind. She knew the elderly couple had names, but they had never told her and she had never asked for them. If they felt it was important for her to know, she assumed they would tell her. Still, she wondered whether they carried English names, as many did nowadays, along with their Indian names.

The sack, now full, arched her back so she took her time returning to her cabin, stopping often to rest. Since it had developed into a beautiful day, and not yet late, Annie decided to put up the nuts and return to the river to fish for a while. When she returned, she made her offering on the water, baited her hook, and cast the line into her favorite deep hole. Once again, she saw the man on the other bank. She could have sworn he had not been there when she had arrived. As always, he waved and smiled. She did likewise. One of these days, she vowed to herself, she would find out his name and why he appeared whenever she did. It occurred to her that the man's presence could make one feel uncomfortable, but she had never once felt that way.

Before long, her rod tip jerked. Setting the hook, she reeled in a good sized large-mouth bass. Taking the hook from its mouth as gently as she could, she touched it lightly on its head and thanked it for its life. She wrapped its body in dry grass, then placed it in a canvas bag, which she used as a creel. When she returned her line to the water, she cast upstream and let the bait wash down past some rocks. Since there was no strike, she repeated the process. Then, suddenly, the line stopped. It was either hung up on a rock, or a fish had taken the bait. She let it sit for a moment and then the line began to move again . . fast! Now she knew there was a fish running with the line. This time, when she set the hook, it felt like she had hooked a log. Her rod bowed into a "U" shape. Annie's heart jumped! A big fish! She felt their spirits join. Their battle was predictable, for the fish would run the river for a while, then Annie would retrieve the line and be in control for a while. This went on for some time. The fish soon tired, but so had Annie. It had turned into a battle of wills. Eventually, Annie's will won, and, as she brought her opponent to the bank, she could not believe her eyes. It was the largest rainbow trout she had ever seen. After removing the hook, Annie spoke to the large fish, saying, "You are a strong and brave warrior. You have earned the right to live and fight another day. Return to your family with pride, and tell your story of the battle. I honor you."

She placed a small bit of tobacco into its mouth as an offering of peace, and returned it to the Long Man, its home. While she watched the fish's wake as it swam to the middle of the river, her gaze caught sight of the man on the other side. He was smiling and giving her a "thumb's up" sign.

Apparently, he had been watching the entire battle, and seemed pleased they had called it a draw. Annie smiled all the way home. Not only had the river provided her with her supper, but it had also given her some fun and excitement.

CHAPTER 18

WE ARE REALLY MANY PEOPLE WALKING AROUND IN ONE BODY. AS WE GROW, WE CHANGE IN MANY WAYS, AND WE REQUIRE DIFFERENT THINGS THROUGHOUT LIFE. AS ONE DOOR CLOSES, ANOTHER OPENS.

—The Elder

A storm moved in, bringing swirling winds, but little rain. It brought down dead trees, one not far from her cabin. Taking advantage of this, Annie spent the next two days cutting and storing wood. Along with the hard labor came sore muscles. Everything seemed to hurt, from her eyelids to her toes. Since preparation for winter happened this way every fall, Annie knew this kind of pain could not be helped. The work kept her strong and lean.

When she grew satisfied that she had a good start on winter, she loaded her truck with wood and headed for the Elder's house. She had earned a day of rest and relaxation in the company of good friends on this sunny day.

When she arrived, the Elder and his wife were sitting on the front porch peeling apples. As Annie climbed out of her truck, a look of concern crossed the faces of the Elderly couple. They must have seen she held herself stiffly and moved a little more slowly than usual. When she reached the porch, the Elder asked, "Have you been hurt Granddaughter?"

"No, Grandfather. I'm just sore from cutting wood. Seems every fall, my body complains more and more," she said, taking the seat he had indicated with a wave of his hand.

"Well," he said, "as you can see, we all do what we must."

The old woman gave him a playful slap on his hand, saying, "Now, Old Man, the next time you are wolfing down one of my hot apple pies, you can feel you have earned it."

They all laughed, and Annie asked if she could help.

"Only if you promise to take some of these apples with you. We really have more than we can use," the old woman said.

"Yes," the Elder contributed, "that way, I will have fewer apples to peel."

Annie picked up an extra knife that lay on a small table between them, and joined the apple peeling effort. As they worked, they talked about many things, but nothing serious, which was good for Annie.

Taking a break with hot cider, Annie asked how they were going to preserve so many apples. "Some," the old woman explained, "I will make into apple butter. Some will go into pies, of course, and some will be baked with brown sugar. But most, we will string, once sliced, and hang from the rafters to dry. That way, we can have apples all winter."

The Elder's wife showed Annie how to core, slice and string the apples. As a child, Annie had seen her own

Grandmother do this, but had not paid much attention to the process. Annie still regretted not learning more from her own grandmother. Like many young girls, she believed she would marry and move away from the farming life, and into the perfect suburban house, where all of her food would come from supermarkets. "Well," she thought, "things don't always happen as children dream they will." She paused, reflecting, "Do children still dream? Do they see a future for themselves? Lord knows, they seem to be much smarter than they were in my generation, or in my parents' generation."

Because Annie was no longer joining in the conversation, the Elder asked, "Your thoughts have gone elsewhere; where are you, Granddaughter?"

"I was recalling my childhood. It was a good childhood, Grandfather. I...wonder about the children of today's world. Is there a good life ahead for them?"

"This, I do not know, Granddaughter. I hear of great things happening in our world, and I see other things happening that are not good."

"What things, Grandfather?" Annie asked.

"Well," he said, "it seems to me there is not as much time anymore for the little ones. With both parents working, or single parents trying to make ends meet, the children, in many cases, are raising themselves. There is a saying in our culture that goes like this: 'It takes a man and woman to create a child, but it takes the whole village to raise it.' That bond is no longer strong in towns and communities. Everyone is just looking out for themselves."

Annie nodded her head. With her seven children, she understood the concept of needing a village to raise them.

He continued, lifting his chin toward his wife, "When we were children, if a child ran hungry, someone in the village fed it. If a child ran cold, someone brought him in around his or her fires. If he felt fear, someone held him until the fear was gone. It did not matter whose child. Everyone looked after everyone else's children. Life was precious, and everyone worked together to preserve it, for the young and old alike. Children were respected and shown great love. This was how they learned respect and love for all life."

The old woman spoke up, adding, "Another part of the circle, you see."

"Yes, Grandmother," Annie said, her mind still deep in thought.

Annie went back to peeling apples, but her mind worked on the problem of how to save the children. No one spoke for a long time, for they were all contemplating the same problem.

Soon, Annie spoke, saying, "Grandfather, can I help in the future of the young ones? My own grown children, and their children, do not understand the world in which I live. In fact, sometimes they do not want to hear about the things I have been taught. Their world is made up of computers and space travel. They do not want to learn the past to prepare themselves for the future. How do we teach them to balance the world of today, the world of the past, and the world of the spirit? How do we teach them to seek truth?

"I have been blessed because I was guided to you. Your teachings have given me the ability to open my mind, not only to my ancient memories, but also to the depths of the human spirit. You, Grandfather, told me this was a gift. But you also told me that this gift held no value unless it could be passed on to others; and with this, I agree. How do I do this when they do not want to hear, or when they just look at me as if I was a crazy old woman?"

"Are you so sure they do not hear?" he asked. "Maybe when you speak, you are not looking deep enough into their souls. If you plant a hundred seeds, and only one grows, then the circle continues. Those who hear will then wish to seek out their own ancient memories and learn, more of the ways of the Great Mother, or the natural world. This desire to learn will lead them to seek an understanding of the spirit world. Once they have found comfort in this, they will, in turn, plant seeds. Do you understand, Granddaughter?"

"I think so, Grandfather, but I must give this more thought," Annie responded.

"True, you should," he agreed. He then asked a question she had never asked herself. "When you were--oh, say, twenty or twenty five years of age, would you have felt ready to accept my teaching? Would you have permitted yourself to be lead by the guides that walk with you now?"

Annie said nothing, but held his gaze, so he continued, "I do not believe you would have. You were being prepared for this journey, but at that time, you were not aware of it because your energies were being used to raise your children and build a life for yourself and for them. When you look at individual lives on a larger scale, you will see that we are each really many people walking around in one body. As we grow, we change in many ways, and we require different things throughout life. As one door closes, another opens. Only those who fear the unknown become locked away. Those who, like yourself, are seekers, accept the open doors. This is how your wisdom is built.

"How do we reach the young ones?" you ask. "One small seed at a time. It may lie dormant longer than you would like, but, when the time is right, it will grow. Neither you nor I can force it. When people are ready, they will then begin to seek answers. That is what you and others, whose seeds are growing, can do to help...just be there for those who want to learn."

Annie's attention was drawn to the old woman when she said, in almost a whisper, "The cocoon is becoming a butterfly." The look in her eyes when she looked up at Annie made Annie's heart almost burst with love and admiration for this beautiful, tiny woman, who, at the moment, did not look old at all.

CHAPTER 19

YO, BROTHER COYOTE, I AM HONORED TO MEET YOU.
—Annie

Fall lingered that year. Cold Maker could not seem to get a good grip on the land. Sunny, cool days kept Annie in the woods, gathering the Mother's fall bounty. On one of these perfect days, she had taken her basket, a small spade, a canteen of water, and a happy heart to look for wild ginger. Leaving her dogs at the cabin, she started walking, with her eyes focused on the ground. Like most of the times when she went into the forest, she forgot the hour, this was especially true in her own woods. She had learned every tree and rock well enough so that she could navigate in the dark, almost as well as in bright daylight. Even as a child, Annie had no fear of the darkness.

Annie walked most of the morning, and found a couple of wild potatoes, but no ginger. It was getting a bit late in the year to gather roots. No matter, the day sparkled around her.

Over the past few years, coyotes had begun to move into the mountains. Annie had never seen one, but now and then, she could hear them on the mountain behind her cabin, talking to one another in the night. She had occasionally seen their tracks after a rain or in the snow.

Guessing the time to be around noon, Annie reviewed her position, and gathered that she had come further from her cabin than she had intended. A bit tired and hungry, Annie took a seat on the forest floor, beside a small spring. She peeled and ate one of the potatoes, but she still felt hungry. She ate most of the other potato, leaving a few bites on a flat rock by the stream. She also left a bit of tobacco as an offering.

As she turned to start home, she saw a movement in a laurel thicket. Annie immediately froze in place, as she had learned to do as a child, and let her sense of sound do the searching for her. Her eyesight had grown weaker with age, but she had been blessed from birth with exceptional hearing and she had honed it so perfectly that she could hear a snake crawling in sand.

Annie remained frozen in place for what seemed forever, then there came a light rustling in the leaves. Moving only her gaze toward the sound, she saw a furry ear, then a black nose. Her first thought was, "It's only a dog," but when the animal's head turned, she saw the eyes of a coyote—'The Trickster,' as it is known in Indian lore. It's ears, eyes, and nose were seeking out the source of scent. Annie did not move even an eyelash, her breathing growing shallow. When the animal finally began moving, it looked like a ghost floating in midair. It did not move toward her, but veered off to her left as if to circle her, loping similarly to a wolf, which always circles right to left when investigating. Annie held her position, despite the cramping in her muscles. Her excitement growing, she knew the animal must be able to hear her heart beating in her chest.

When the coyote had moved behind her, walking in and out of the brush and trees. She became a little nervous, but not really fearful. Finally, from the corner of her eye, Annie saw the animal's head and shoulders. It had made a full circle around her, apparently still not sure about her. Moving around to see her front, it stepped out of the thicket. Annie now had full view of this beautiful, red-gray creature. Gazing directly at her, it stopped completely. Annie knew that looking an animal directly in the eye is perceived as a threat, but she could not help doing so. She wanted to share her spirit with the coyote. She focused her eyes on his. He did not show signs of feeling threatened; but returned her gaze. As she had done with other animals, many times before, she sent the coyote a message, from her mind to his, assuring him she honored him as a friend, a brother. She felt that he understood, for neither she nor the coyote lowered their eyes. Mesmerized; Annie could feel herself being pulled into his very soul. This coyote was real: flesh, blood, bone and fur...not a spirit, as she felt the wolf had been.

Annie forced her mind back to herself, and decided to speak. Never taking her eyes from his, she said in a soft and low voice, "Yo! Brother Coyote. I am honored to meet you. I am called 'Woman Who Walks Alone.'"

At the first sound of her voice, the coyote took a few steps back, not showing signs of fear, but appearing a bit confused. Annie stopped speaking, and when he had seemed to settle down, she turned to leave, saying, "I must go now. I hope we will meet again. Go in peace, Little Brother."

After a few steps, she looked back over her shoulder and saw the laurel thickets moving. She knew he had entered the thicket, but still watched her. Delighted, she wanted to sing, dance and skip like a child; but she walked on in a slow, even manner, to avoid scaring the creature.

As daylight turned to dusk, Annie quickened her pace and headed for home. Just before stepping out of the woods into the clearing around her cabin, Annie heard a lone coyote singing his evening song. Somehow, Annie felt he sang for her. Turning and looking back toward her mountain, she said softly, "Good night, Little Brother."

CHAPTER 20

*AFTER SOME REST AND REJOICING WITH THE ANCESTORS,
I WILL RETURN IN SPIRIT TO YOU.
THERE IS SOMETHING YET UNFINISHED.*

—The Elder

The following morning, Annie arose to a cold, drizzling rain, which showed signs of giving way to snow at any moment. That's the nature of the mountains; one moment rain; the next moment, snow; and maybe before the end of day, full sunshine. Annie loved the old timers' theory on weather: 'If you don't like it, hang around a little while, and it will change.'

Coming from a farming family, Annie had learned to pay close attention to the weather. Even though she no longer lived on a farm, the farmer mentality had been bred into her, and she would not willingly forget it.

The unpredictable weather made Annie's restlessness

return. Her indoor work finished, she found it too wet for any outside work. The birds visiting the feeder in the yard told Annie more about the weather than the weather man, and winter birds flocked to its rim this morning. The birds expected a change, and come, it did! The thermometer on Annie's front porch began to drop. The rain turned to ice; then to heavy, wet snow. Annie's instincts told her this would be more than the usual light and easy snow. By early evening, the power lines and trees could bear no more.

Earlier in the day, Annie had double checked her supplies: food that could be eaten without cooking, batteries for her radio; candles; and fuel for her lamps. She would do fine without the luxury of electricity. Around seven o'clock that night, the power lines finally gave up. Annie guessed the whole county had been pitched into darkness. Speaking to her dogs and cats, who wanted nothing to do with the blizzard raging outside, she said, "Here we go, boys and girls. It's probably going to be a long night."

True to her prediction, the blizzard gave Annie no rest. The winds blew with such force that no trees carrying the extra weight of the snow had a chance...they came crashing down under the weight. Over the sound of the wind, Annie could hear a crack and thud. Jumping with each crack and thud, she feared that a tree would soon come crashing down on her tiny home.

At first light, she surveyed the damage. Trees were down everywhere. Electric lines had been downed, either by heavy ice and snow, or by trees falling across them. For two days, the storm continued. Although the wind subsided, the snow did not retreat for some time. Annie kept an ear to the radio, awaiting updates on the storm. She knew that everyone for miles around hung in its mercy. Nothing would move until road crews and emergency people could get out and start clearing snow, removing downed trees, and repairing power lines. Now, it became a waiting game.

Not until four days later was the lane cleared, and the power crews didn't make it to Annie's part of the country for another three days. With so many feet of snow on the ground, walking proved difficult. Annie finally broke through the deep snow to check on her neighbors and on the summer cabins she tended during the winter months. She found no major problems anywhere. Although the storm had been the worst one of the century, no lives were lost. As far as Annie knew, everyone came through the storm without serious mishaps, and perhaps, a little more respect for Mother Nature.

Once the wind died down and the trees held up, the woods took on a stillness like no other silence Annie had experienced before. Annie found it physically draining to walk in the deep snow, but she wanted to be in it, to feel its power. She spent the next several days plowing through the surrounding woods, thankful that her two large dogs were willing to break a trail of sorts for her. On these walks, she found signs of deer, bear, coyote, rabbit, turkey and grouse. They, too, had emerged from their dens and covers, looking for food. For them, Annie carried apples and nuts on each of her daily forays into the woods. Though not intended as survival food, Annie felt her small gifts would be appreciated, and would let her wild, free animal friends know that she had come through the storm unscathed.

The sun soon returned, whipping the heavy snow into retreat. Except for the downed trees, all would soon be back to normal, and spring would enter, well nourished by the melting snow. Annie could hardly wait for spring, and for her next visit with the Elder and his wife. Were they okay? Would the roads be clear enough for the drive? She didn't know, but had to try.

On the eighth day following the storm, Annie could wait no longer to check on the old couple. Leaving her cabin with a prayer on her lips and a kind word to her old truck, she found the main roads clear, but still icy in places. When she reached the turnoff to the Elder's cabin, Annie found her passage blocked. The snows in this cove had retreated very little, and apparently, no one had begun clearing the roads. Fear rose in her heart. When she looked up the old, long, narrow lane, she felt she viewed the end of the world. The lane, steep with switch backs, almost looked impassable. Still, it was only about two miles to the short trail that led to the Elder's front door. If she took her time, she could make it. She determined not to turn back now!

Forcing her way further through the snow for what seemed like hours, Annie saw the cabin. Standing strong, smoke billowed from the chimney—this was a good sign. Reaching the porch, which had been swept clean of snow, Annie brushed snow from her boots and jeans and came up onto the porch. The old woman opened the door, and looked at Annie with a touch of sadness in her eyes. The expression caused Annie's fear to resurface. She invited Annie to come in and warm herself while she prepared some hot tea. Annie stepped inside and let her eyes adjust from the brightness of the sunlit snow to the dim light in the cabin. When she could see, she looked toward the Elder's rocker, expecting to see him sitting there wrapped in his beautiful blanket. He was not there. Annie turned as she heard the old woman entering the room. She carried only two cups of tea.

"Grandmother," she asked, with that nagging fear now filling her voice, "where is Grandfather?"

As the old woman handed Annie the cup, she said, "He is ill and has taken to his bed. I have been treating him with my medicines, but he seems to have given up, and giving up is an illness I cannot treat. That must come from within."

"How long has he been sick?" Annie asked, adding, "I was just here a few days before the storm, and he seemed fine."

The old woman began to explain in her broken English, with a weariness in her eyes and voice. "He was out offering his morning prayers, as the cold rain began. When he returned to the cabin, his clothes were soaked clean through and he was shivering. I helped him out of his wet clothes and got him warm, but the chills would not stop. I have done all I know to do, and still he grows weaker."

Annie did not want to risk offending the old woman by suggesting that the Elder should be taken to the hospital. They sat before the fire and drank the tea. After a few moments, Annie asked, "Grandmother, is there anything I can do for you or Grandfather?"

Surprisingly, the old woman responded, "You could try to convince him to go to the Indian hospital. I fear I have done all I can, and he will not hear such a suggestion from me. He now has a rattle in his chest, and I am afraid he has...," she was searching for the right English word, "...pneumonia."

Annie's heart froze. Pneumonia, if neglected too long, could not be warded off effectively by the very young or the very old. Taking the old woman's hand, as much for her own comfort as for the grandmother's, Annie said, "I will try. Is he awake?"

They both went to the small bedroom near the kitchen. The room, heated by the wood cook stove, held warmth and comfort. The Elder looked up at them as they entered the room. He smiled weakly, and patted the edge of the bed, gesturing for Annie to sit down. Pale and ashen, his face held shadows covering his eyes. Stricken by the results of his illness, Annie tried not to show a reaction. She smiled and greeted him with great love in her voice. She knew the Elder had been a large man in his youth, but now he looked so small! Although little more than a week had passed since the old man fell ill, the illness had quickly taken its toll. He spoke mostly in a whisper, his lungs not receiving the air he needed for speech. Annie carried the conversation, talking about the great blizzard, and about how well she had fared. She talked of the oncoming spring. Then, finally, she said,

"Grandfather, I am worried about you, and your wife is beside herself with anguish. If not for yourself, but for us, let me get some help up here so we can take you to the hospital. Your wife loves you and she feels she has done all she can for you. Will you go? Please, Grandfather."

He looked over at his wife, who had sunk down into a chair at the other side of the bed, then looked back at Annie. Finally, he said, as strongly as he could, "No. I am tired, Granddaughter. The ancients are calling for me to join them. It is time, and I could use the rest before my next earth walk," he said, with a boyish smile. "You may mourn for me if you wish, but do not be sad for me. My life has been good, and I have been blessed." Exhausted, the old man could not continue. He seemed to drift off to sleep.

Annie rose from the side of the bed, leaned over, and kissed his forehead. She knew, at that moment, that she would not see him alive again. She fought back the pain in her heart, for he would not approve of her sorrow. Annie turned, not looking back, and went into the kitchen. The old woman followed, and removed from the stove a poultice for the Elder's chest. Meanwhile, Annie heated some water and made them each another cup of tea. The old woman returned from applying the poultice and sank into a kitchen chair, saying that he was sleeping and that the poultice would help his breathing. She sipped her tea, then spoke slowly to Annie, "Granddaughter, could you do something for me?"

"Of course," Annie said. "Anything."

"First, could you please bring in more wood from the shed?" she asked. "I have used all that was on the porch."

"Of course," Annie answered as she rose to go to the shed. The old woman took her arm, and Annie sat back down.

"Second, could you go to the town and find my niece and her husband, whom you have met before? I will need their help." She explained where they lived.

Annie brought in armload after armload of wood, until her arms ached. Then, she hugged the old woman and said she would return quickly with the old woman's niece.

"No, they have a truck, and can get here on their own," she explained.

"Okay," Annie said, "but I will return to help you in any way I can."

Again, the old woman shook her head. "No, Granddaughter. We have learned to love you as a Granddaughter, but it is our custom that only blood kin should be in the house when the old man is called away. Please try to understand, and do not be hurt. A ceremony must be performed to help guide his spirit; one which none but family can observe. Do you understand, Granddaughter?"

"Yes, Grandmother, and I will honor your custom, of course, but my heart and spirit will be with you," Annie replied.

"Thank you," said the old woman. "Now, go. It is growing late, and I feel that he will be gone before the next sunrise."

Annie kissed the old woman lightly on the cheek and started the long trip down the snow-filled lane. Her tears turned cold as they rolled down her cheeks. How strong were these beautiful people, who accepted the will of God and the ancient ones! Annie wished she possessed that kind of strength, but right now, she felt sad and alone. Try as she might to hurry, her legs felt like logs. The walk to her truck seemed to be an eternity. She forced the tears from her eyes so she could see, and headed east toward town. She found the niece's house with little trouble. At her knock, she was invited inside out of the cold. The Elder's relatives remembered Annie, and asked her to have a seat. Annie thanked them, but declined, immediately explaining her reason for being there. The relatives showed strength, and were not shocked by the news. They thanked her and said they would go right away. When Annie reached the bottom step of the porch, she turned and said "My heart goes with you. I am sorry to be the messenger of such bad news." They only smiled again and thanked her for coming.

Reaching her cabin in the dark made her heart ache even more. For the first time, being alone grew to be almost more than she could bare. Annie had only her animals, and she was thankful for their company. Needing to reach that deep, dark void of meditation, Annie built up her fire, sat cross-legged in front of it, and began searching for the comfort of warmth, letting her mind drift. She stayed there through the rest of the night, with her dogs lying close beside her. Sometime in the predawn hours, she received a message from the ancients. Grandfather had joined them. His journey had been easy and swift, for which Annie was thankful. Sometime after daylight, she went to her bed and drifted off into a deep sleep. The Elder came to her in a dream, speaking to her soothingly, "After some rest and rejoicing with my ancestors, I will return in spirit to you. There is something yet unfinished." Then, his face faded and the blackness of deep sleep engulfed her. When she awoke, the dream lay still and clear in her mind. She did not understand the Elder's message, but when she began to question it, his voice returned, as if he were in the same room, "Do not question it!"

CHAPTER 21

GRANDDAUGHTER, THE ELDER ASKED THAT I GIVE YOU SOMETHING. HE WISHED FOR YOU TO HAVE THIS AFTER HIS JOURNEY HERE WAS FINISHED.

—The Grandmother

The month stretched long for Annie. She respected the customs, and did not make contact with any of the Elder's family during their mourning time. Annie mourned in her own way. Her heart grew heavy with the loss, but to her surprise, sadness did not overwhelm her as she had expected. Maybe the Elder's last request to her, that she not be sad, had created an impact.

Preparing for her spring work proved difficult for Annie. She wanted only to roam the woods or sit on the banks of Long Man or stand on her boulder looking toward the mountains where this beautiful man had walked. Strangely, she had not yet shed a tear for him; she had shed tears only for her own loss, fearing that the he would not approve of her sadness.

The Elder had left Annie more than his teachings. He had left her a sense of strength, and the wisdom to know the difference between self-pity and sadness. After all, Annie continued on her earth walk, and, as the Elder had told her in the dream, something was yet unfinished. Now, she must wait until he returned to reveal to her what this meant.

The pain in Annie's heart diminished as the weeks passed. She began to put her back and her mind into gardening. She would continue to plant a few extra cucumbers and tomatoes for him; she could not let go of this small gesture of love for the Elder. This was the time of year when she felt the presence of her own grandfather as she worked the soil. She found his presence to be very comforting. Annie had not spoken of the Elder nor of her 'spirit time' in the mountains to anyone—not even to her own family. It had been a personal and private part of her life, yet she felt that her grandfather knew of it and had kept her secret.

On a clear and warm morning, as Annie headed for her garden, she received a small message telling her to return to the Elder's cabin, for the old woman wished to speak with her. Without hesitation, Annie put away her garden tools, changed out of her work boots and into her moccasins, prepared a bag of nuts to bring as a gift, and began her journey. When she arrived, she found the old woman sitting on the front porch, looking up toward the mountains. As Annie reached the steps, the old woman looked down at her and said with a smile, "Woman Who Walks Alone, thank you for coming."

Annie had learned over the years, that when nurtured and respected as a gift, our minds can carry our thoughts and wishes, not only to God and our guides, but also to others.

Telephones are quick and handy, but the mind can do the same thing; it just takes a little practice. This had always tickled Annie, as it did now, remembering an incident with the Elder.

The couple had gone into town for a celebration of some kind. While in town, the Elder had asked someone to dial Annie's phone number, so he could talk to her. Annie had been outside working close to her cabin when she heard the phone. She ran to answer it, saying, "Hello," and heard nothing. She said, "Hello," again, then heard the Elder say, "Ha! These things really do work." He was laughing! Annie interrupted his laughter, saying, "Grandfather, I thought you did not like these things!" Finally, he settled down and spoke into the phone, with his mouth a little too close to the mouthpiece. "Well, I don't," he said, "but I must admit, it is faster than trying to reach you the old way, and I knew you would be surprised."

Annie let the memory fade and returned her attention to the present. "Grandmother, are you well?" she asked.

"Yes, thank you," she answered, waving her hand toward another rocker. "Come, sit for a while. I am glad you are here." Annie thanked her and sat down. For a long while they gazed quietly out across the valley onto the distant peaks beyond. Annie had many questions, but she held her tongue until the old woman opened the conversation.

Finally, looking over at Annie, the old woman said, "You have been well, Granddaughter." It was not a question, but a statement. This wise old healer could look at a person and know if their heart, mind, or body were sick. She also knew that any of the three could be painful and could cause the other parts to weaken and die.

Now Annie was in a dilemma. She knew and understood the old ways and customs. In this case, when someone crossed to the other side, his or her name could never be spoken again. But, since Annie had never known his name, was it permissible to speak of him at all? Although such questions were pressing on her, she did not want to be disrespectful. The old woman seemed to know the thoughts going through Annie's mind, for she took her eyes from the mountains, and, looking at Annie, said, "You have questions of the Elder, Granddaughter? If so, do not be afraid to speak of him. You will not be showing disrespect. Now, I have set tea to steep. Please go inside and bring us a cup, and then we will talk."

Annie did as she had been asked. After drinking her tea, the old woman spoke again, slowly and carefully. "Granddaughter, the Elder asked that I give you something. He wished for you to have this after his journey here was finished." She drew out from her apron pocket a black stone that had been worn smooth and polished from years of handling. It reminded Annie of a "worry stone." The old woman looked at the stone a moment, then handed it to her. As Annie received it in her hand, she felt a sense of comfort she had not known for a long time. Cool to the touch, the stone felt more precious than a diamond to Annie. As she turned it over and over in her hand, the old woman explained that the Elder had carried it from the time he had been a small boy. She did not know why, but the stone had held great importance to her husband.

Though the stone did not reveal anything in particular, Annie knew that it held life and memories of the earth. It also held memories of the Elder, and a part of his spirit had been absorbed by it. To Annie, it was a great gift, which she felt the Elder had made a part of her spirit medicine. She would hold it in great honor. For many years, Annie had worn a medicine bag containing her spirit medicine. Removing the bag from her neck, she kissed the stone lightly and placed it inside the bag, where it would be safe and with her always.

When Annie again looked at the old woman, she saw a tear slowly fall from that lovely copper face. "Grandmother," Annie said softly, "I am honored by the gift, and I thank you. I would like to thank Grandfather. May I go to where he has been placed to rest?"

"Of course, Granddaughter. He is resting on the small hill above the cabin."

Annie walked to the hill and found the marker and the stones. She did not feel sadness as she sat down next to the grave, but spoke to the Elder as she did when he was still with them in the body. "Grandfather, I hope you are resting well and that you are celebrating with your ancestors. Thank you for the beautiful stone. It is here in my medicine bag, lying close to my heart. You have shown me great honor with such a fine gift. I also understand why you left it behind for me. Your spirit will never be far away from those who love you. This stone has told me that you will continue to guide me on my earth walk. Again, I thank you." Placing her hands upon the stones covering the grave, she felt comfort and peace, and she knew that he lay in peace.

Annie returned to the porch, thanked the old woman for allowing her to take time with the Elder, and again, thanked her for the gift. Then, as she prepared to leave, she asked, "May I return to visit you and Grandfather again, Grandmother?"

"Well," the old woman said, "I would be hurt if you did not, and I believe the Elder would, too. Come any time you wish."

"It is time for you to plant," Annie said. "May I help you with the maize this year?"

"Thank you Granddaughter, I don't think I can do it alone."

"Fine," Annie said. "I will return in a couple of days to prepare the soil. Is there anything I should bring?"

"Only an empty stomach," the old woman replied, with a chuckle. "I will fix us a fine supper."

"Thank you, Grandmother," she said, then turned down the trail and headed for her truck.

When she returned two days later, as she had promised, she found a kitchen full of good smells. There were pots and pans everywhere. Every kind of Native American dish she had ever heard of had been prepared or was in process. The old woman bustled around the kitchen, then went outside to stir a bubbling pot of corn, cooking over an open fire. Annie could not believe her eyes at all the food. "Grandmother, surely all this food is not just for the two of us!" she exclaimed.

"No," the old woman said. "I have decided we should have an 'old-way' corn planting feast. I have invited friends and family to celebrate with us. I hope you do not mind."

"Of course not, Grandmother. I am honored that you have included me. Now, what can I do to help?"

The old woman looked at her with a twinkle in her eye, saying, "You just watch over the cooking food and I will return in a short while." She then retreated to the bedroom, closing the door. When Annie went out back to check the pot, she looked toward the patch where the next corn would be planted. To her surprise, it had already been turned and worked smooth. She had no idea who had done the work, but she knew that the old woman was not capable of such heavy labor.

Annie returned to the kitchen to find a beautiful woman in full Cherokee dress, from the "old way," as she called it. The dress was made from a heavy cotton twill, the color of blue sky, with a full, ankle length skirt. At the bottom, ribbons representing the four corners of the earth had been stitched to encircle the skirt: red, for east; blue, for north; black, for west; and white, for south. The shirtwaist was also decorated with these colored ribbons, at the neck and around the cuffs of the puffy, long sleeves. Around her neck, she wore two necklaces of trade beads and corn beads, sometimes called Job's Tears. On her feet were soft doe-colored deerskin moccasins. She had braided her beautiful, white hair, wrapped the braid, and pinned it atop her head. She moved with such grace, it was like looking at a vision. Annie just stood and stared, then found her voice enough to say, "Grandmother, you are beautiful!"

The old woman's face flushed as she thanked Annie.

Looking down at her own appearance, realizing she had come to work, Annie had worn suitable attire: jeans, a denim shirt, and work boots. She had brought along a change of clothes to wear after the planting, but they were not appropriate for a feast.

The old woman saw into Annie's mind, and said with a smile, "You must look festive also, Granddaughter. It would please me if you would wear the blouse I have laid out for you on the bed. I think it will fit."

Annie retrieved her nicer jeans and moccasins from her truck, and went into the bedroom to change. The old woman urged her to hurry, for the guests would be arriving soon. Annie found on the bed, a simple, but beautiful yellow blouse, decorated with ribbons of many colors hanging from the shoulders. It fit her perfectly! She quickly changed, brushed her hair, and returned to the kitchen. The old woman turned around, wiping her hands on her apron as she inspected Annie. She smiled her pleasure.

The first arrivals were the old woman's niece and family. Annie started to relax, because she knew these first guests.

Then, as if someone had opened a flood gate, people appeared from all directions—some on foot, some in trucks and cars, and one young man and his sister, on a horse. Most were full-bloods, but some were mixed-bloods, so Annie no longer felt out of place. The men began laying out planting sticks, while the women carried pots and pots of food to the yard. There were many children, from babies to teenagers. There were old men and women, and people Annie's age.

The old woman beamed from ear to ear when Annie asked her just how big was her family? "Granddaughter," she said, "you know I never had children of my own, but some of these folks I helped bring into the world, so they are all my family. Now, stay close beside me and learn."

Everyone made a circle around the worked earth, each with a planting stick in hand. The old woman explained that the maize would be planted the old way. "Put the stick into the ground up to that mark, then place in Mother Earth three or four seeds. Cover the seeds, and pat the ground smooth."

A bag of seed corn was brought out from a shed, and smaller bags were given to everyone. Each, in turn, walked from right to left in the circle, filling their smaller bags from the larger one. When everyone returned to their original places in the circle, an old man and woman went to the center and offered a prayer to the Creator and Mother Earth, asking for a good harvest. Since the prayer was given in Cherokee, Annie understood only parts of it. During the prayer, she heard repeatedly the name "Selu," the Corn Mother. When the prayers were finished, they separated into two groups, one at each end of the field, and began planting the rows, working toward one another. Annie watched the people beside her, to make sure she did it properly. Then, taking her stick, she sunk it into the ground up to the mark, and placed three seeds into each hole. With so many people working, it did not take long before the whole patch had been planted. This is fun, Annie thought to herself. Everyone laughed, joked, teased, and had a good time.

One young couple, obviously in love, became the object of most of the teasing, and they took it in good fun. Annie could not remember when she had seen so many happy people, but then, she had always avoided crowds. Somehow this was different, and her heart grew so light, she thought it might fly from her chest. The passing of the Elder had been hard on everyone and they needed some happy times. Annie looked toward the mountains to the west, just as the sun began to drop behind them, and thought she saw the Elder's face smiling down. Yes, Annie knew he approved of the event, and felt pride for his people.

The chill of the evening started creeping into the cove and people wrapped shawls, blankets, and jackets around themselves. Children and babies were growing quiet, snuggling into their mothers' or fathers' arms. Fires were lit, blankets were spread on the ground, and people began to settle down. Most of the food had been eaten and the women were cleaning up. Then it was story telling time.

First, an old woman told the story of Selu. Everyone knew the story, of course, but some of the young ones were just beginning to learn it. Then, an old man told a hunting story that was quite funny. The story told about the first time he and his brother set out to hunt alone as young boys. According to the story, the two boys decided to climb a tree that hung out over a game trail. The boys knew that the deer used this trail to go to the water. Just as a large buck moved almost directly below them, they became so excited that the storyteller's brother slipped and fell out of the tree, almost on top of the deer. The brother was not hurt, but the deer could still be running, to this day.

Later in the day, the brothers found turkey tracks, and decided that hunting turkey would be easier than hunting deer. So, they began to sneak through the woods, as they had seen their uncle do. But they soon found the going to be more difficult than it looked, and that turkeys were not as dumb as some people thought. The two brothers were as quiet as they could be, thinking they were getting close to the large bird. They would see the bird...then the turkey would vanish. This went on for most of the afternoon, but they had decided that they would not go home empty-handed. Finally, at sundown, they had moved to within a few feet of their prey, and started feeling cocky, when, without warning, three large tom turkeys came flying out at them from the undercover. They thought they had been following just one turkey, when, all the time, there had been three. The three turkeys had been leading the boys in a circle until they had tired of the boys' foolishness, and decided to make them the prey. They attacked the boys with wings flapping and feet kicking. "Well," he said, "they did not stop running 'til they got home." To avoid embarrassment, they told their parents they had not seen any game. To this day, neither one of the brothers is fond of turkey hunting.

When everyone stopped laughing, the old man told riddles to the children. As Annie looked around at the faces glowing in the firelight, she could not imagine that any other way of life could be so full, and she felt blessed to be a part of it. Let the rest of the world play with their electronics, and end up bored. This is the way the Creator meant for people to enjoy life.

Annie had no idea of the time. The moon had climbed above the mountains; the fires had burned low; and the babies were all asleep. Voices had become whispers, as people talked amongst themselves. Soon, farewells were exchanged, and people began drifting away. Everyone left full, happy and tired. Annie had caught the old woman drifting off to sleep. She helped her into the cabin, took a quick look around to make sure everything had been washed and put away, changed out of the borrowed blouse, said her 'Good nights,' and headed down the path toward her truck. She felt drunk with pleasure, experiencing the natural high that can't be imitated by anything else. She hoped she could drive home without getting pulled over, for how could she explain her drunken state, without having drank a single drop? This would be a new challenge for the law!

CHAPTER 22

I AM KNOWN AS 'OTTER WOMAN,' MEANING THE MEDICINE OF WOMAN, OR, IN MY LANGUAGE, 'TSI YA A GE YU.'
—Otter Woman

Spring began shifting into summer. Tourists poured into the mountains once again. Annie continued to be helpful as she had always tried to be, but that old nagging tension grew, which drove her to seek out solitude whenever she could. She had not been to Wolf Mountain all winter. She felt the need to visit again, hoping the woman with the digging stick would be there.

Finding the same spot where they had met before, Annie made herself comfortable and waited. Ever since leaving her truck at the bottom of the mountain, Annie had felt eyes on her. This did not bother her; she felt at ease in the mountains. If she were, indeed, being watched, it could be by her four-footed or winged friends. If they wished to show themselves, they would. She let her mind fly free, absorbing the beauty around her. The forest smelled of earth and green--she could smell the green.

Out of nowhere came a voice, saying, "Sister, it is good to see you."

Annie jumped. She had not heard anyone walk up behind her. Turning abruptly, she saw the woman with the digging stick. Not knowing her name, Annie responded by saying, "Tsi lu gi" (welcome). "I am sorry, I do not know what you are called."

They both smiled and sat down. The woman laid her digging stick and gathering basket beside her, and said, "I am known as 'Otter Woman,' meaning the medicine of woman, or, in my language, 'Tsi ya a ge yu.'"

"Well," Annie said, "My Cherokee is not very good, so may I just call you 'Otter Woman?'"

"Of course, sister. Have you been well through the winter?"

Annie nodded, replying, "Very well, thank you, and you?"

"Yes," Otter Woman responded. "I spend the winters drying and curing the herbs I use for healing. It is a busy time for me, but I am happy when I can once again roam the woods to gather. Do you know of healing herbs?" she asked.

Annie shook her head. "No, I do not have the knowledge of such things, but I hold admiration for those who do."

Otter Woman studied the younger woman for a moment, her dark eyes looking deep into Annie's. Then she said, "You are a seeker, I feel, and are kin of the animal world, not of the plant world."

Annie looked down at her hands, saying, "I suppose that's true. I can't remember a time when I was not drawn to all animals, domestic and free."

Otter Woman then let her eyes rest on Annie's left side, then her right, saying, "And I see two of your animal guides never leave you."

Annie was not sure she had heard the woman correctly. After a moment, she asked, "You can see these guides?"

"No," Otter Woman said, "but I sense them. The wolf, a female, walks on your right. The bear, a male, walks on your left. Is this not so?"

"Yes," Annie said, "but I'm not sure when they began doing this."

"Well," Otter Woman asked, "when were you first aware of them?"

"After I moved into the mountains," Annie replied, "when I had been here a few months. When I was roaming around different areas, I would get a strange feeling, or things would happen that I could not explain."

"This frightened you?" the woman asked.

"No," Annie said, "it confused me. Then, in time, I was directed to an Elder of the native tribe. He was very wise and a fine teacher. He guided me through these confusing times, and I began to understand my spirituality, and the ways and teachings of these mountains. There is great energy here, and I have remembered many, many earth memories. The Elder taught me how to pull forward my ancient memories and, in doing this, I was shown a different way of living—one I had never before taken the time to see."

As Annie spoke, the woman sat quietly, nodding her head with a knowing look on her face. "These spirit guides that walk with you...they were given to you by the Elder?" she asked.

"No," Annie said, "they have been with me all my life, but I did not recognize them until I came to walk on the path which I now follow. I feel blessed that the kind Creator has shown me this path in our beautiful world, and opened my mind to all it has to offer. The Elder instilled in me the desire to learn about the past. He said, 'Learn about the past, for it will be the future.' He taught me that, although this can sometimes be painful, I must never permit anyone to pull me away from seeking and learning."

"Come," Otter Woman said, "I wish to show you something." They rose and walked on the ridge line for some time, then dropped into a small glade. The glade, about the length of a football field, but wider, brought a strange elation within the soul of Annie. There, in the center of the grass-covered cove, lay a small lake, which bore a color Annie had never seen in any of the lakes around there or anywhere else. It had to be the clearest lake she had ever seen, and released a faint odor of sulfur. Annie had been raised on black sulfur water, so knew the odor very well.

From the small rise where they stood, Annie looked down and saw animals of various kinds, drinking or bathing at the lake. Annie started to speak, but the woman placed her finger to her lips, to signal silence. They sat down and watched the animals. There were four-footed, feathered, and scaled animals, all together, but showing no signs of aggression or fear. After some time, Otter Woman tapped Annie on the arm, and motioned for her to follow. They both rose quietly and walked softly back into the woods away from the lake. Once out of sight of the glade, Otter Woman stopped and sat down. Annie did the same, as she asked, "What was that place? Why were all of those animals there, and why was the coyote not chasing the rabbit?"

Otter Woman laughed and asked, "Sister, do you always ask so many questions?"

Annie also laughed, saying, "Yes, I have many times been told that I do." Annie felt so comfortable with this woman that she wanted to become her friend.

Otter Woman then drew out from her leather pouch, cloth wrapped corn cakes, and said, "The sun is high. While we eat, I will explain."

Annie had brought fruit and water with her. She took the fruit from her pack, and they placed the food between them, and ate in silence for a while. Finally, Otter Woman said, "I will answer your questions only if you promise never to reveal the whereabouts of this glade to anyone, and never to go closer to it than we were today. Will you make me these promises?"

"Yes," Annie said.

Otter Woman smiled, knowing she could trust Annie. "The glade," she said, "is a sacred place, and the lake holds healing waters for our animal relations. They come to this lake when they are sick or wounded. The coyote does not harm the rabbit, because he knows that this is a place of peace. They know if any one of them causes harm to any of the others, the glade will be taken away from them. This knowledge was born to them, for the animals also have been blessed with ancient memories."

Annie then asked another question. "Did humans ever go to the lake for the same purpose?"

Otter Woman smiled, then said, "Perhaps many hundreds of years ago, but not in recent history. This is one place that belongs only to the animals, and they seem to know that. Although they knew we were watching them, they felt no fear, because they knew that we were also there in peace and would not enter their sacred ground. They have seen me many times, and they have never shown fear. As for you, they not only saw you for the first time, but they also saw your spirit guides that walk with you. Animals do not fear humans who have animals as guides. The Creator has given you a great gift, and you must never abuse it. We are all animals in the great natural world. Sister, have you ever felt fear of the animal world?"

"No," Annie said, "but I have felt fear of the human animal."

"Ah, yes," Otter Woman said, nodding her head. "That is because, I'm sorry to say, mankind is the only animal that destroys for pleasure or power. I fear that this condition is growing worse all over the world--not only what we do to one another, but also what we do to our Mother Earth. I know of people who are fighting to save her, and this is good. When we save our Earth, we will then be saving ourselves. This is another part of the circle, you see. I believe you and Elder spoke of this many times, did you not?"

"Yes," Annie said, "but how did you know? Did you know the Elder before his earth walk was completed?"

"Not in the physical world, but we knew each other," she said, simply. Then she added, "He has asked me to help you continue your truth-seeking. We did not meet by accident."

This revelation did not surprise Annie. She had learned that everything happens for a reason, and she had accepted this.

Otter Woman then rose, leaving an offering of corn meal and a couple of corn cakes. She embraced Annie, saying "We will meet again, but now I have work to do. Stay well, my sister." She turned and vanished into the woods. Annie also prepared to leave. She left an offering of tobacco and a few pieces of fruit. Then she turned down the trail and hiked back to her truck.

CHAPTER 23

LEAVE THE FIRST THREE PLANTS FOR SEED. GATHERING THE FOURTH—AND THE MOTHER WILL CONTINUE GIVING THE PLANT'S HEALING POWERS TO MANKIND.

—*Otter Woman*

Annie drove home with her thoughts still back at Wolf Mountain. The Otter Woman was flesh and blood, or so it seemed. Still, Annie could not understand what she had meant when Otter Woman said she did not know the Elder in the physical world. Did they communicate only by way of mind and spirit? Were they bonded in some way from a previous life. A mere mortal, Annie had learned how to reach the edges of the spirit world, but had never entered it completely. She did not know why; maybe because of fear; maybe because her inner power was not strong enough; or maybe because the spirit world would not permit it. Since she didn't know the reason, Annie chose not to dwell on it. If she were ever to go there, she must trust the forces that would guide her.

Annie had learned to trust her personal guides, for they had shown and taught her many things. Not all of the lessons had been pleasant, but they were given to her for a reason. She had seen and felt pain, not only in herself, but also in others, and she had to believe that some good comes from "bad" experiences. There are times, she felt, when God and the guides must seem cruel, yet the resulting outcome of the experience would be only kindness; some call it "tough love."

Everything is connected, Annie reasoned, and it is really very simple. Only the human animal tries to complicate the circle of life. Instead of harmony with the world, mankind creates havoc, and for what? Stress and ulcers, more money, more power? Annie thought that some people probably considered her lazy, since she never had the drive to become rich or powerful. The wolf does not live as the deer, yet they hold respect and admiration for each other. Why can't man respect the differences between cultures and beliefs? Well, Annie did not have that answer, but she felt deeply that this would someday change, and the human animal would, once again, learn harmony. This would not be an easy turnaround, but Annie felt that harmony was possible. For now, she would continue to learn, and, along the way, she would help anyone to learn who so wished. The Elder's words came back to her, "Plant one small seed at a time."

Annie returned to Wolf Mountain several times throughout the summer. The healing lake fascinated her. She kept her promises to Otter Woman: she would never reveal its whereabouts nor go closer to the sacred ground than the two of them had gone together. When she went to the healing lake, she walked quietly to the overlooking hill, and sat for hours watching the animals. They looked in her direction, but never paid much attention. Sometimes, on these visits, Otter Woman would find Annie, and they would sit and talk, or Annie would walk with her as Otter Woman gathered herbs. Otter Woman explained to Annie how respect for the plant world was as important as respect for the animal world. When she found a cluster of herbs or roots, she passed up the first three plants, and took only the fourth plant in the group. She would then move on to another cluster, always leaving an offering of corn meal in the soil from which she had taken the plant or root.

"In this way," she explained to Annie, "the Mother will continue giving to man the healing powers of plants. Always leave the first three for seed, and thank the ones you take for their lives."

It was a simple form of conservation, practiced by the American Indian for thousands of years.

"Greed," Otter Woman explained, "only produces hunger, sooner or later."

Annie understood this principle. When she gathered wild food, she always left some of the plant, not only for seed, but also for the animals and birds that depended on the food for survival.

Annie's garden grew bountifully that year. She shared its yield with her neighbors and friends. Sometimes, they traded beans for tomatoes, corn for peas, or cucumbers for squash. The trading worked well, and made for a wider variety of foods to store for the winter.

It had been a week since Annie's last visit to the Elder's cabin. She gathered tomatoes, cucumbers, squash and lettuce into baskets and left her cabin as the sun came peeking over the mountains. When she reached the Elder's cabin, she found the old woman in the maize patch, declaring war on the weeds. Her back turned to Annie, she bent over her hoe. Annie could not be sure to whom the old woman spoke—to herself, to Mother Earth, or to the weeds—but she certainly was getting her point across. Her voice would rise high, then low and guttural. Since the old woman spoke her native tongue, Annie could not understand the actual words. Still, she felt blessed that she was not a weed in Grandmother's corn patch!

The old woman had not heard Annie's approach, so Annie spoke softly when she drew near. "Grandmother," Annie said, "do I see before me a Warrioress, fighting an enemy?"

The old woman turned, and a touch of embarrassment crossed her face. Then, smiling shyly, she said, "Woman Who Walks Alone, I am afraid you have caught me at a weak moment of anger. It seems for every weed I remove, two weeds take its place, and they bring in their reinforcements over night."

Annie laughed, saying, "Now, Grandmother, what would the Elder say if he heard you speaking to the Earth Mother in such a way?"

Wiping the sweat from her brow, she said, "Oh, I'm sure the old man is sitting around the council fire, right now, clicking his tongue at me."

Annie did not respond to the old woman's comment. Instead, she took the hoe and joined the battle, saying, "Grandmother, you rest for a while and cool down before you get sick," Annie gave time for the old woman to cool her temper and her body!

The old woman went to the back porch and sat in the shade, watching Annie bend over the hoe. Soon, she entered the cabin and brought out cool apple cider, and as the two of them rested, Annie spoke of Otter Woman without saying anything about the lake.

"Grandmother," Annie said, "I'm not sure how to look upon this woman. I feel close to her, yet I really know nothing about her nor how far my questions should go."

The old woman gave her a soft smile and asked, "Do you fear offending her?"

"Maybe," Annie said.

"Perhaps, like yourself, she is not comfortable with talking," the old woman said.

Annie just looked at her, not sure what the old woman meant. They sat in silence, sipping their cider. After a while, Annie asked, "Grandmother, what did you mean about talking?"

"Well, Granddaughter, there are times when I am made to believe that you have taken a vow of silence."

"Yes, I guess there are times when I get lost in my thoughts, but I do not mean to seem distant with anyone," Annie said.

Annie finished hoeing, then went to the hill to speak with the Elder. After the proper greeting to one who is on another plane, she asked, "Grandfather, your wife brought forward something I have not given much thought to. She says I have become quiet, maybe even distant. Is this wrong?" Of course, there was no response, but Annie felt he had heard her.

Returning to the porch, Annie found the old woman dozing in her rocking chair. As Annie sat down, the old woman spoke, without opening her eyes. "Thank you for your help today, Granddaughter. I seem to be so tired these days. I wonder if I will be able to gather the corn when it is ready."

Annie gazed closer at the small woman. Over the past few visits, she had thought the old woman seemed thinner and a little drawn. "Grandmother," she asked, "Do you feel ill?"

"No," she said, "just tired. The ancients are waiting for me and I am more and more looking forward to joining them."

"Grandmother, do not say that!" Annie's eyes grew wide and her heart felt fear. "You are just tired today, and you will feel better after a good night's sleep."

The old woman gave Annie a quick glance, saying, "I do not sleep. For over seventy years, not a night went by that the Elder did not lie beside me. I no longer know how to sleep alone."

Annie said nothing else. She knew the old woman had made up her mind. She had grown tired of putting up the front that she was not suffering without the Elder. That kind of bond cannot be separated for long. Annie looked into her eyes and gave her a smile that said, "I understand." Annie rose, bent down and kissed the old woman on the cheek, and walked down the path to her truck. She knew then that the old woman saw her own impending death as a celebration.

CHAPTER 24

GRANDDAUGHTER, I WANT TO SEE DANCING LIGHTS IN THOSE EYES...THIS IS A CELEBRATION!
—The Grandmother

As summer passed into fall, Annie found herself seeking out solitude more and more often. The silence of the woods became addictive to her; the more she had, the more she wanted. She avoided people whenever she could, escaping into the forest like an animal, much the same as the woman who had carried her name before her. Annie was not the same woman she had been when first she came to these mountains. She had walked from one world, into another. She had found a peace she had never known. Though there were those who tried to take that peace away, she fought to bring it back. She may have been forced to bend at times, but she never broke; instead, with each new confrontation, the stronger she became. Her spirit guides grew, and before long, her circle became full and strong. The Creator held that circle together with love.

Though her years now numbered over fifty, when she spent time in the woods, on a mountain top, or lying beside the river, Annie felt young and full of life. Her heart and spirit were free to soar as did the hawks. The wolf who walked on her right had become her sister and friend. The bear who walked on her left had become her soul mate and protector. This relationship was not one-sided, however. When Annie sensed danger, she pulled the wolf and the bear inside herself to keep them out of harm's way. At other times, Annie felt as though they had stepped in front of her to keep her from walking blindly into dangerous situations. Great trust had grown among these three, and Annie felt truly blessed. She felt that if her earth walk ended tomorrow, no one should feel sorry for her, for she had been given much more in life than she had ever expected.

Annie finished harvesting from the garden just as the nuts began to fall from their mother tree. Autumn turned out to be as busy as summer had been. Those who take their living from the land are always busy; preparing the land for planting; the planting itself; gathering wild fruit, berries, mushrooms and roots; cutting and stacking wood and gathering nuts in the fall; and preserving the harvest. The cycles continue year after year.

It would soon be time to harvest Grandmother's corn. Annie looked forward to the harvest festival. Everyone would bring food this time, and the harvest would go quickly, with all working together. The old woman had helped Annie make herself a festive blouse for the event. Beautiful in corn yellow, the colors of the corners of the earth were stitched to the collar and around the long, puffy sleeves. Annie loved it and hoped to one day pass it on to one of her daughters.

The day of the harvest festival, Annie baked squash from her garden and cooked a pot of green beans seasoned with salt pork. As with most gatherings, there would seem to be more food than they could eat, but this impression would be proven wrong, as it had been in the past.

Annie arrived at the Elder's cabin early to help set up the serving tables. The old woman's beautiful gown hung loosely on her frail body. Because of her failing health, she did not bustle around as she had at the planting festival. She sat on the back porch, visiting with all who came, carrying a smile on her face to hide her weary heart. Annie's own heart grew heavy as she watched the old woman. She knew this would be Grandmother's last harvest. The old woman saw the sadness in Annie's eyes, and called to her to come and sit beside her. She took Annie's hands and said, "Granddaughter, I want to see dancing lights in those eyes. This is a celebration, and, like it or not, you will have fun, you hear?"

"Yes Ma'am," Annie said with a smile crossing her lips. She returned to her work remembering the old woman could wield a sharp tongue when the need arose.

When the participants finished arriving, there were twice as many people as there had been at the planting festival. Annie guessed that they all knew what she knew, and because they all loved Grandmother, they wanted a last chance to be close to her. The same old man and woman from the spring festival called everyone to the corn field. On the west side of the patch, four circles were formed around the two older people. Each circle represented the four cycles of the seasons. The children were in the first circle, closest to the center; young women were in the second; young men, in the third; and the Elders, in the fourth. The old couple told the story of Kana'ti and Selu, the story of the origin of game and corn, followed closely by a song of thanksgiving. The ceremony closed with a prayer to the Creator and Mother Earth.

Everyone then divided into two groups, with each group going to a different end of the field, just as they had done during the planting. They worked toward one another, pulling the ears of corn from the stalks and placing them into large burlap bags. On every fourth stalk, a few ears of corn were left for the animals. A portion of the best ears were shucked and placed in mouse-proofed barrels for the following years' seed corn. Another portion was set aside for the feast: it would be roasted in the hot coals of the many fires they had built for that purpose. The old woman said she would not have any use for the corn, and insisted that the rest be divided equally among those present. Her announcement worried everyone. They had come to enjoy the feast, and had given their labor from their hearts—they did not expect payment of any kind. Out of respect for Grandmother, they honored her wishes, but with sad hearts. Once the dividing of the corn ended, the old woman's voice rang out high and strong, "Let the feasting begin!"

Annie and Grandmother's niece filled the old woman's plate and carried it to where she sat on the porch. The old woman gummed the food and smacked her lips, and decided it was the best food she had ever tasted. Children danced for her as she clapped her hands to the rhythm. A young woman with a beautiful voice sang in Cherokee for the group. Annie saw tears fill the old woman's eyes as she listened. Stories were told—some were about the old woman, who would blush and laugh as she listened. At some point, it occurred to Annie that this was not just a celebration of corn; this was also a celebration of Grandmother's upcoming journey. "What a wonderful way to say 'goodbye!" Annie thought. Instead of tears and wailing, there rang out laughter and song. This event would not take place over a lifeless body; the celebration in honor of an old woman's earth walk was being given in her presence. Grandmother knew her walk would soon be over, and she wanted to greet her ancestors with a smile on her face and a happy heart.

The feasting ended a little after midnight. Everyone said their goodbyes, but Annie, who held back, making sure, before she left, that everything had been washed and put away. Some of the men offered to return in the morning to take down the tables. The old woman's niece and family were planning to spend the night with her. Once she had finished checking the cleanup, Annie knelt in front of the old woman. Their eyes met, but no words were spoken. Their spirits mingled, their hearts touching. No words could have brought them closer together at that moment. The old woman knew that Annie understood her need to go to the Elder. Annie rose, kissed the old woman on top of her white head, and left. Annie did not look back, for she did not want the old woman to see her tears.

Two days later, Annie received the message: Grandmother had gone on her journey.

In the weeks following the old woman's departure, Annie had busied herself to avoid dwelling on how much she missed the Elder and the grandmother. She felt a great sense of loss, but knew that the two were happily together again. The appropriate time of mourning had passed. Annie had gathered nuts and restocked her wood supply, and had finished preserving the last of the fall foods. The winds told her it would be an early winter; she felt prepared for whatever was to come.

CHAPTER 25

*SHILOH CAME TO ME TO CARE FOR; TO HELP EASE THE
PAIN OF LOSING THE ELDER...AND NOW HIS WIFE.*

—*Annie*

Earlier in the fall, Annie had found a large hound dog in the woods, lying beside a tree. At first glance, the brown, black and white dog had looked as though it had no life; but when Annie moved closer, she had heard a whimper from the dog's swollen throat. While examining the starved animal, she saw fang marks in its chest. Annie recognized the marks as snake bites, and, though she had little hope for the dog, she lifted it to her shoulders and headed for her cabin. Despite the dog's starved state, it's large-boned body proved quite heavy. Annie had to stop several times to catch her breath. When she reached her cabin, Annie laid an old blanket close to the stove and packed the dog's neck and chest in ice. She spoke softly to the dog, hoping to ease its pain and fear. Annie's other dogs—who had also been lost, starved strays—nosed and whined around the wounded newcomer. The injured dog opened her eyes, but did not move. After a couple of hours, her shivering stopped. Annie stayed beside her through the night, replacing the ice bags as they melted. Around dawn, Annie fell asleep. Awakened by a cold nose nudging her arm, Annie found one of her dogs trying to get her attention. She patted his head and looked over at the wounded hound. To her surprise, the young female had pushed herself up and fastened her gaze on Annie. Stroking the dog's silky ears, Annie said, "Well, Little Girl, I see you have decided to live. Welcome."

Annie put away the ice packs, and saw that the swelling had diminished, and the angry-looking fang marks had begun to close. She wished she could take the dog to the healing lake, but that would mean carrying the animal to the water, and she had promised not to enter the sacred ground. She offered the dog some water from a bowl; the dog took a few swallows. Later, she would see if she could eat some bread soaked in milk.

As the day passed, the dog slept. Toward evening, she tried to eat a little bread and milk, but swallowing seemed to be difficult. After a few more days, the glazed look in the animal's eyes vanished, and, though her legs were unsteady, she pushed herself up into a standing position. As the dog regained strength, Annie noticed that when she reached out, she shied away from her hand. Annie took this as a sign that the dog had been beaten. She abandoned the idea of trying to find her owner. When the dog showed sure signs of living, she decided to give her a name. She couldn't go on calling her Little Girl, for the animal was not little, as evidenced by the pain in Annie's shoulders, five days after carrying her home!

Sitting with the dog's head in her lap, Annie said, "Well, young lady, what shall we call you?" The dog rolled her big brown eyes up at Annie; they were no longer full of fear, for she now understood Annie would not hurt her. Annie thought for a moment, then the name popped into her mind: 'SHILOH.' The name fit well, for the poor dog still shied away from strangers. She would not even join in the other dogs' play when Annie took them on walks. Though she constantly grew stronger, Shiloh still hung close to Annie's legs.

Cold collared the winter; however, it passed with little snow. Annie's cabin, now more crowded than ever, had grown to be an obstacle course of four legged bodies. At night, Annie had to shuffle her feet to keep from stepping on tails or long, floppy ears. In time, Shiloh flourished, gaining weight and growing a shiny coat. Her eyes flashed brightly, and she began to play with the other dogs.

However, as she gained strength, Shiloh's behavior changed. While the other dog's stayed close to the cabin, Shiloh roamed in the woods. Early one spring day, Shiloh returned from the woods with a rabbit displayed proudly in her mouth. Annie's heart sank. The hound had been bred to hunt, but Annie had hoped that the instinct would not return, for she had grown to love this dog. Annie did not hunt animals, and she strongly disapproved of certain forms of hunting. Yet, she understood that some folks needed to hunt in order to feed their families. She also knew that many animals starved during winter months, due to overpopulation, because so many natural predators had been hunted to extinction. The animal world tilted and rocked, with no balance; and because this balance had been disrupted, a lot of wildlife lived in a see-saw situation. There were no easy answers to the problem of wildlife conservation in the modern world. Annie pondered the problem at hand: she did not believe in restraining animals with chains or pens. The instinct to hunt, as natural to this dog as breathing, knew no easy solution. The pattern would not be broken without also breaking Shiloh's spirit, and Annie could not do that. Even as she searched for a solution, deep down, she already knew the answer.

Annie had met hunters who took very good care of their dogs. She decided to talk to some of them about Shiloh. A few years before, Annie had met a woman whose husband's hunting dogs were well fed, provided a large, fenced playyard, and given access to a heated barn during the winter. The hunter seemed to love all of his dogs. When Annie took Shiloh to meet these people, they recognized her as a well-bred hunter. After they heard Annie's story, they agreed to accept Shiloh into their pack, and assured Annie that she could come visit anytime. This made Annie feel much better, and she decided she would, indeed, visit Shiloh. When Shiloh went through the gate to join the other hunting dogs, Annie's heart stood still with apprehension. The other dogs came running, tails wagging, voices baying, and noses inspecting. Shiloh turned once and looked back at Annie as if to say, "Thanks, these are my kind, and I'll be just fine."

Annie missed the hound on her walks, but she knew Shiloh was happy and would now be able to do what she loved to do. She visited Shiloh often. In the beginning, Shiloh would come running to greet Annie, but eventually, Shiloh broke the bond. Now devoted to her pack and to the people who cared for her, Shiloh's story had a happy ending. She had touched Annie's life for a few months, and Annie knew she had made the right choice.

Now she had to ask herself, was this dog sent to her to help ease the pain of losing the Elder and now his wife? In her heart she felt they had placed the wounded animal in her path to distract her, to help her.

Annie had not returned to the Elder's cabin all winter. She did not know why, but thought, perhaps, she secretly feared the memories would be too painful. One day, when the dogwoods were just beginning to bud, she felt a strong urge to go to the cabin. She took gifts of nuts and tobacco, just as she had always done. She headed for the cabin, not sure what she would find, nor how she would feel once she arrived. As she neared, the first thing she noticed was the absence of smoke billowing from the chimney. Missing nothing as she neared the cabin, she could tell no one had been there all winter. The windows and doors had been boarded up, indicating that no one wished to take over the primitive cabin. Not many young folks wanted to live in the old way. The old rocker still sat on the front porch. Annie sat down, looked up toward the mist-covered mountains, and let the memories of the cabin and its people flow into her. She let her mind work backward, from the last time she had been here, during the harvest festival, to the first time she had met the Elder. Very clearly, she heard the laughter, the crackling fire, the stern voice of the Elder when he tired of her questions, the soft voice of the old woman the day Annie had received her new name. She heard it all, but instead of tears, she found a smile on her face. She realized one does not cry tears of sadness when given a gift—and what a gift she had been given! Annie would carry this gift throughout her earth walk, and maybe, into her next one.

    Annie walked around to the back of the cabin and stood, looking at the dried corn stalks. Deer tracks were everywhere; the deer had found the corn that had been left for them after the harvest festival. She walked to the hill, where the old woman rested peacefully beside the Elder. Annie sat between the rock cairns that covered the couple's resting places. She placed the tobacco at the head of the Elder, and the nuts, at the head of the old woman. Annie spoke softly, unsure whether she spoke to herself or to them, but she felt better for it. The pain subsided in her heart. Ready to leave, she asked the Elder about the unfinished business of which he had spoken before his passing. A voice sounded, strong and clear inside her head, "There you go again, pushing for answers. Will you never learn? I am still celebrating with my ancestors. When the time is right, you will know." Annie bit her tongue—she had to learn to stop being so impatient.

CHAPTER 26

WOMAN WHO WALKS ALONE, I AM PREPARING FOR MY RETURN AS I PROMISED. I WILL SOON GIVE YOU A CHALLENGE. MAKE READY.

—The Elder

Annie never again returned to the Elder's cabin. She knew the Elder would contact her when he felt the time was right, and, besides, the memories were too painful. That cabin and the surrounding mountains represented where her spiritual quest had begun, where she had been given a great gift. Her greatest gifts had come with life itself: her own life given to her by her parents and the life she gave to her children. She placed this new gift of rebirth with the other two, and held all of them close to her heart. These three precious gifts once again revealed her sacred number.

For the time being, Annie knew she must trust in God and in the guides that the Creator had given to her. She had learned that when life presented a situation which she could not handle alone, she had only to ask for help, and the guides would come to her aid and to the aid of those close to her. Annie was at peace with her way of life, and she questioned it less and less. Her ancestors had guided her here for a reason; of this she had no doubt. And, she must wait to see what they wanted her to do with the gift. She understood now what the Elder had taught her: To be of value, a gift must be passed to others.

Spring and summer passed in much the same way as before, except for one thing: Annie found herself needing to spend more time alone. The Elder and the old woman were never far from her thoughts, day and night. Annie's dreams became clearer, and she remembered her dreams more easily. A strong believer in dreams, she knew they carried messages, so she placed them in her memory for future reference.

One warm, summer morning, the three hawks circled and called to Annie as she worked in her garden. She understood the message, so she immediately left for the mountain. When she reached the boulder, she sat quietly for some time, before the hawks came to her. She greeted them, and as they flew overhead in a circular pattern, Annie heard the voice of the Elder.

"Woman Who Walks Alone," he said, "I am preparing for my return as I promised you. Stay alert; be aware of everything; and take nothing for granted. I will soon give you a challenge. Make ready." Then, the voice and the hawks were gone.

Annie started to speak, but held her tongue, telling herself, "Do not question this." The longer she sat, thinking about the message, the more angry she became. Her voice rose from her throat, louder than she had expected. "Wait a minute," she yelled, "you can't do this to me! You can't leave me hanging like this! I need to know more. Please, Grandfather, you can't do this!"

She did not hear his voice, but a thought entered her mind, which she recognized as the Elder's, Oh, yes I can! Her mind's eye saw him chuckling and giving her that familiar sideways look. Annie grew so furious that words flew from her mouth before she could stop them: "I hope you are enjoying this. You are playing with me, and I don't like it! Your amusement is at my expense, you know!" She stomped her foot like a spoiled child, then looked around, taking a deep breath. Thank goodness no one was around to witness this outburst, she thought. If anyone caught her arguing with a spirit, they would probably lock her up in a rubber room.

Annie did as she was told. She remained alert, and looked for a challenge. If the Elder played with her mind, she reasoned, he must have a purpose. She became filled with determination to pass this test, just to show him!

Fall came early. Annie had been slow getting her wood restocked. She scoffed at herself; for in this ninth year of her being in the mountains alone, she knew by now what it took to get through the winters...and that too much time roaming in the mountains could cost her some cold nights. Annie sharpened her chain saw and put her back to the task, day after day, until she knew with confidence that she had enough wood to see her through until spring.

In February, a heavy snow laid on the ground for over a week. Annie again grew restless. She felt the urge to explore mountains other than those close to her. She remembered climbing a certain mountain that stood several miles from her home, so when the snow melted, she drove to its base and began hiking. The trail stretched up distinctly before her, but, even with the sun, a cold breeze tugged at her jacket. She breathed deeply, allowing the cool air to fill her lungs.

Reaching the top, she sat down, and looked out over a deep valley and the mountains beyond. As she ate her lunch of cheese, crackers, and jerky, she let her mind roam, not thinking of anything in particular. The trail, a part of the Appalachian Trail, which starts in Northern Georgia and ends in Maine, was heavily used from spring through fall. But this time of year, however, it was rare to see any hikers. She had not seen nor heard anyone, and except for the animals, Annie felt she had the whole mountain to herself.

Since starting the climb, Annie's restlessness had subsided, and she felt adventurous. After eating, she left the trail to venture deeper into the woods. Walking a few hours, she noticed her shadow growing longer, and decided to turn back. When she turned around, she had a feeling of apprehension. The woods around her looked different, somehow. But, Annie knew she had been walking east, so she simply turned toward the setting sun and began her hike back to the trail and to her truck. As Annie walked on and on, the joy of the day gradually became replaced by a heaviness in her chest. For the first time, the woods felt ominous. The sun had dropped behind the higher mountains, and she thought how quickly the temperature drops to freezing in the deep, mountain woods. Still not concerned, Annie continued to shake off her uneasiness, for she expected to find the trail soon.

But, as Annie walked on, finding nothing familiar, small doubts began to slip into her mind. She had not seen an animal, and even the winter birds had grown quiet. Then, a growing sense of being really alone brought on her first touch of fear. Annie had never been lost in the woods in her life. She could hardly find her way around a city block, but in the woods, she had always felt at home. Since she could not locate a trail, she decided to find a creek to follow, guessing that the creek would eventually bring her to a road. Although she had not come prepared to spend the night, she did have matches and a knife in her backpack; if necessary, she could build a fire and a makeshift leanto. She would be fine.

With darkness still at bay, she continued looking for a creek or the trail. She found neither. Annie had a hard time admitting she was truly lost, but she finally had to accept it. Just as she began to scout the area for a place to spend the night, she heard a movement in the heavy brush. She investigated the sound, and found a black bear walking away from where she stood. She followed it a few steps, until it stopped and turned, looking directly at her. She held her breath, waiting to see what the bear would do. It took a couple of steps toward her, never taking its eyes from hers. Annie calmed herself by opening her mind. Perhaps the bear was trying to tell her something. The bear once again started ambling away from her. Annie sensed that she must follow him, but she did not move. The bear did not stop, but looked back over his shoulder, as if to say, "Come on, if you're coming!" Annie followed the bear, and, within fifteen minutes, she found herself on the trail.

With amazement, Annie stood still; then turned to look down the trail. There sat the bear on his haunches, watching her. Slowly, she began to walk toward him. He did not move until she came close, then he rose and made off down the trail.

The bear led Annie, walking about three feet ahead of her. Then, entering a switchback, he disappeared from sight. When Annie rounded the curve, she did not see the bear, but there, before her, walked the Elder. He stopped, turned, and smiled at Annie's disbelief. Tears rolled down her face, as she looked past the Elder at her truck. She could say nothing but, "Thank you, Grandfather." The Elder's smile broadened, and he waved, stepped off the trail, and vanished from sight. On the edges of her vision, Annie saw the back of a black bear, heading toward the deep woods.

Had Annie's eyes played a trick on her in the near darkness? Her mind thought they had, but her heart knew better. The Elder's spirit had returned, taking the form of the bear to bring her out of the woods. He had kept his promise.

Annie had trouble sleeping that night. She tossed and turned, catnapping, but never really reaching sleep. In one of these drifting-off periods, she heard the Elder speak to her. "First you pushed for answers, now you push for dreams. That is why you do not sleep."

Annie turned on her side, and asked aloud, "God, does the Elder know everything?" The answer came back: Yes, now he does. Annie smiled to herself, and slipped into sleep.

For the next two nights, Annie did have dreams. She and the Elder were sitting in his cabin. He began telling her what he wanted her to do. The dream, unclouded and clear, filled her mind; but the Elder's voice seemed far away. Annie had to strain to hear him.

First, he made sure that she understood all of the gifts that she had been given: not only those from him, but also those from God, Mother Earth, and her spirit guides. When the Elder grew sure that Annie understood, he again made sure she understood the importance of sharing her gifts. She understood, but she had the same question she had asked before: how was she to share this gift? He looked at her from hooded eyes, and said, "You will tell our story."

The dream faded, and Annie awoke to morning, though she felt as if she had just fallen asleep. Over her morning coffee, she asked herself how she could tell the story. She did not consider herself a story teller.

The next two nights were dreamless. She felt the answers were just out of her reach, and this brought complete exasperation. There must be a lesson here somewhere, she reasoned.

One night, when Annie had decided to dismiss the problem from her mind, the Elder returned to her dreamtime. They were again in his cabin. Before he opened the conversation, she jumped right in: "Grandfather," she said, "why do you play these cat and mouse games with me? Why do you give me only half of something, and then just leave me hanging? What have I done to make you act this way? I want answers!"

The Elder spoke softly, but sternly, to Annie. "You want answers, do you? Well, how about looking into yourself for them. The answers are there, you know. You were doing well in finding them before my earth walk was complete. Now you are slipping. Have you grown lazy?"

Oh, Even this man's spirit is frustrating, Annie thought to herself.

"I am not," the Elder said.

Oh great! Now he can read my mind. What next? Annie thought.

The Elder leaned forward, close to Annie's face, saying, "Now, can we get back to what I want?

"Yes, Grandfather," said Annie, humbly. She realized she would have to be more respectful, even in her thoughts.

The Elder pulled back, and spoke again. "As I was saying, I want my teachings and those of our ancestors given to others. You will do this, will you not?'

"I guess so," Annie answered. "but I am still not sure how to do this."

"May I make a suggestion?" asked the Elder.

"Sure," Annie replied, hesitantly. "I have a feeling you have planned this out already."

"Oh," he said, "I had planned it out before I left the

Sleep With The Wolf—Walk With The Bear

earth. You were not yet ready then to be the messenger. Now, my suggestion is this: put our story in the written word—English words—on paper. I want you to write it. The written word is a powerful thing!"

"You want me to do what? I am not a writer! I wouldn't know where to begin...." Annie could say no more. She knew nothing about writing. The very idea scared her to death.

"Well, you think on it. We will talk soon," said the Elder.

Annie's dream then faded, and she slept deeply.

As the days passed, certain words came up and then began to play and replay in her mind: Sleep With The Wolf...Walk With The Bear. Over and over again, like a song one hears and can't stop singing, the words continued in her thoughts. In a phone conversation with her father, Annie mentioned the words.

Without hesitation, he said, "It's a title."

With her father's validation of the words being a title, thoughts of a book began forming in her mind. Could she do it? She had no idea, but the least she could do was try. Her family encouraged her, and gave her full support. After a few days, she sat down with pencil and paper, and wrote the title across the page. That was it. After three hours of thinking, nothing else came to her mind, except, How can you have writer's block when you haven't written anything yet?

That night, the Elder once again entered her dreams. This time, he stood on the boulder of her mountain when she reached him. He never took his eyes from the mountains across the river, as he spoke. "You have a very nice mountain," he said. "I feel strong spirits here. You are having trouble finding the door to open for the words I wish you to write?"

"Yes, Grandfather. I do not feel I am the one to do it," Annie said, regretfully.

"Well," he said slowly, "I was looking forward to my next earth walk. I had even chosen my parents, but now I see you still need my guidance, so that will have to wait a while longer. I will tell the story. You will be the instrument to put it on paper. Is this acceptable to you, Granddaughter?"

And so, the writing began. Day after day, the Elder stood at Annie's side as she typed word after word. They laughed, and even argued, but in the end, he got his way. How do you win with a spirit? When her back hurt and her fingers cramped, he pushed her to continue. Maybe he no longer needed sleep, but Annie was still flesh and blood, and she said so. Whenever she thus appealed to her mortality, he would agree and say, "Your earth walk will be ending, and I would like to get on with my next one, so if you don't mind, we will continue."

Annie's earth walk does still continue. What lies in her future? What lessons has she yet to learn? Only God, the ancients, and her guides know for sure. This much, Annie does know: because of these mountains, the Elder, the old woman, and her animal guides, she is now more open to receive the gifts and the lessons that life holds for her—without questions.

Now you ask, how do I know so much about Annie and the path she has walked? I know, for I am she.